The Fetch of Mardy Watt

The Fetch of Mardy Watt

CHARLES BUTLER

An imprint of HarperCollins*Publishers*

To Alison Leslie

First published in Great Britain by Collins 2004
Collins is an imprint of HarperCollins*Publishers* Ltd
77-85 Fulham Palace Road, Hammersmith,
London, W6 8JB

The HarperCollins website address is:
www.harpercollins.co.uk

1 3 5 7 9 8 6 4 2

Copyright © Charles Butler 2004

ISBN 0 00 712857 6

Charles Butler asserts the moral right to be identified
as the author of the work.

Printed and bound in Great Britain by
Clays Ltd, St Ives plc

MRS WATT CAME into the bathroom without so much as a knock.

"There's no such thing!" she complained.

Mardy jumped hastily off the bathroom scales and reached for a towel. "What did you say, Mum?"

Mrs Watt was carrying a rolled-up copy of *Fave!* She waved the magazine in Mardy's face. "'How to find your perfect weight and stay there!' Do they realise that growing children read this nonsense? The perfect weight! There's no such thing."

"If there was, I'd be two stone over," Mardy concluded gloomily. She stepped past her mother, through the scented bath steam to the door.

"There's nothing wrong with the body God gave you, Mardy. Now then, have you seen my hair dye?"

Mardy discovered it behind the spare toilet roll. She knew what was coming next.

"If you want to worry about anyone's weight, worry about your brother's," said Mrs Watt. "He's a shadow of himself."

"Yes, Mum. That's different."

"Different because it's real."

Mardy pulled a face. When her mother mentioned Alan it always made her feel guilty, though she didn't know why. Probably guilt was just another way of worrying, like Hal said.

"Are you going to the hospital today? I'll come with you – I'd like to."

"I was going to drop in on the way home from work," said Mrs Watt briskly. "But if you want, I'll wait for you here. Just make sure you're back by 4.15."

"I will."

"I don't want to be late."

"Of course not," muttered Mardy.

Her mother made it sound as if Mardy hardly ever visited Alan. Surely that wasn't true?

She mulled it over as she walked the mile to school. Mardy usually went the longer way, skirting the park because of the men who sat there drinking cheap vodka, the ones her mother called Undesirables. The park railings thrummed by and, in between bushes, she saw the raked soil where flowers were set to grow in spring, the paths and sludgy leaves. She saw the men too, lying on benches by the War Memorial – all stubble and urine and wheezing self-pity. They seemed not to notice the weather or even their own sad condition. But they must, she thought... they *must*. It made her angry that they could waste themselves like that while Alan lay unconscious week after week. And over the railings tinkled a thin, beaded string of notes, plucked from an instrument that Mardy could not name. The music crept between the railings and followed her some way down the street.

Alan had been in the General Hospital for three months now. He was in a coma and nobody knew why. At first he had been very ill indeed. Her mother had not said so, but Mardy knew she had believed Alan would die. For days the house had been deathly still. Even to turn on the television would have felt heartless. Besides, there was nothing Mardy had wished to see or hear, except that Alan was well again. Photographs of her elder brother – humorous, elegant, ironic – sat on every mantelpiece. It had been a terrible time.

But Alan had not died. "He's a fighter, that one," the doctor had told Mrs Wall, the day his breathing had first stabilised. "We thought he was fading, but he just refused to let go. I don't know where he gets his strength from."

Mrs Watt knew. She said that Alan had his strength from her.

"He'll never leave us," she said.

Alan had not left them, but he had not come back either. Ever since, he had hovered between death and life. Sometimes, when Mardy visited, he seemed barely more than an object, a half-wrapped parcel in folded blankets. On other days his sleep seemed so light that she would not have been surprised to see him sit up and say "Morning, Spud! Did I doze off? I could murder a bacon butty!"

Mardy turned up the collar on her coat. She was walking down a long straight road with two lines of plane trees and Victorian, stone-clad houses behind them. The road itself was spacious and clean, and might have been called handsome but for the cars cluttering it on either side. But Mardy could never love its unbearable straightness and muscle-aching length. It made her feel small and lacking in purpose. Behind, the iron railings of the park were still visible; before her was the school itself. The two held her between them like a pair of cupped hands, and would not let her go.

As usual, Mardy stopped halfway down the street to call for her best friend Hal. Hal's was a large stone house too, but where most had a patch of grass and a flowerbed in their front garden, his had gravel and a fountain. The fountain was made of a green, glowing, jade-like stone and on a grey day like this was the brightest object in sight. Hal's family called it their "splash of colour".

Hal's mother was outside, raking the gravel. She looked up as Mardy's watery shadow crossed her own and smiled. "Upstairs," she said, with a jerk of the head. Mardy went through the kitchen, where Mr Young and

Hal's little sister were debating the nutritional value of Honey Loops, and so to Hal's room.

Hal was tilting a tray of school books into his backpack.

"How's our project going?" Mardy asked. "I want a full report."

"See for yourself," said Hal, nodding to a computer screen.

Mardy looked. One half of the screen displayed a photograph of a sheep in a field. In the other a second sheep (which Mardy vaguely recognised) was sitting in a railway carriage with some knitting. Above this picture Hal had printed "THE SHEEP OF THINGS TO COME?" in lurid letters, dripping blood.

"I know it's not exactly right for the 'Ethics of Cloning', but I got carried away."

"It's great," Mardy said encouragingly. "Just Yarrow's thing. You're a marvel, Hal, a marvel."

Hal looked relieved. "I'll work on it some more tonight."

They left the house – Mardy leading, as was her right. At primary school Mardy and Hal had not been close. There, Mardy had been the queen of her own court, the most popular child in class. Hal, at best, had been her court jester. Popularity was a strange thing. Mardy had been neither the prettiest, nor the cleverest, nor the nicest person in her year. She dressed well enough, but was not spectacularly fashionable. She was barely above average in art, in sport decidedly below. Yet she was the one whose friendship counted – and whose dislike could send a child to lonely exile at the fringes of the class. Mardy could not have explained this herself, but had seen no reason to question an arrangement so much to her own advantage. She had assumed it would go on for ever.

Then came secondary school. Most of Mardy's friends were heading to Marshall Community. Juanita, Carrie and Charlotte were all going there, along with half a dozen more of her hangers-on. The only one of her group destined for Bellevue School was Hal Young. At the time she had thought of Hal as a kind of consolation prize. Not that Mardy had been worried. True, she would miss her old friends, but soon she would be enthroned at the centre of a fresh set of admirers.

Yet Bellevue School had remained indifferent. Mardy's face was just one among hundreds. Most of her new classmates had arrived with friendships intact and felt no need of her. She was not disliked, no one bullied her – but no one sought her out either. When it came to picking teams, she found herself relegated to the middle of the list.

If Mardy had been a weaker girl, or a more truly conceited one, she might have coped far worse. As it was, she was soon reconciled to her modest position.

It was even a relief not to be continually looked to for her opinion. There was always good old Hal, she told herself, if she needed to practise her leadership skills. Next to Alan's illness, what did any of it matter?

The plane tree road was longer than ever today. By the time Hal and Mardy reached its end a sharp hissing rain was falling.

Hal consulted his watch. "It's 8.58 already, Mardy." He was always precise about time, and kept and spent it carefully. "Better give Hobson's a miss."

Mardy paused, but only for a moment. She thought about her perfect weight briefly, but habit got the better of her. "I'll only get the plain bar this time, not the double chocolate."

She was already halfway through the newsagent's doorway.

When Mrs Hobson saw her she reached automatically for the double chocolate Nut Krunch Bars, while Mardy found the right money. "Just the plain today," Mardy told her virtuously.

"On a diet, Mardy?" Mrs Hobson smiled knowingly.

"Certainly not!"

But Mrs Hobson's knowingness was proof against indignation. "I'll be sure to lay in a stock of low-calorie bars," she confided in a very audible half-whisper. The only other person in the shop – a twiglet in a mini-skirt – turned and looked Mardy over. Mrs Hobson continued: "I know just how hard it can be, believe me. Fighting Temptation."

Hal was waiting by the school gate. "Got your chocolate fix? Then let's go, before you rack up a detention."

Two lates in one week equalled one lunchtime detention and Mardy was riding her luck. They skidded up the empty corridors of C Block to the corner classroom, where Mrs Yarrow was already halfway through the register. Luckily both their surnames came late in the alphabet. A number of children smirked as they came in together. One group in particular – that snooty lot from Bluecoat Primary – exchanged looks as if they were in on a scandalous secret involving Mardy and Hal. It didn't matter that the secret wasn't true. What mattered was being in on it.

Mardy sat in her place and answered Mrs Yarrow in her turn just as if she had been there all the time. She knew how seriously to take the Bluecoat lot. They knew nothing of her and cared even less. It was Rachel Fludd she was interested in.

Rachel was the only other girl who had arrived in the class without a ready-made set of friends. Her family had only just moved to the town, it was said. Rachel herself had a slight accent, pearled with rolling 'r's and lazy, hissing 's's – but it was hard to pin her down. Sometimes, she would make a remark that suggested English was not her first language. She had odd little areas of ignorance, had never heard of

Christmas cards, seemed not to know what milkmen were. But Mardy could never be sure, for Rachel was not communicative, on that or any other subject. She sat by the window as often as she could, and sulked.

Mardy was not quite sure how she had come to dislike Rachel so much. Both were strangers, both a little lonely: they could so easily have become friends. Yet even their likenesses drove them apart. Skinny, and taller than Mardy by two inches, Rachel might otherwise have been her sister. If Mardy had stood in front of a fairground mirror to see her reflection stretched out long and squeezed in thin, that reflection would have looked a lot like Rachel. But that just made Mardy remember how far she was from her perfect weight and she resented Rachel all the more.

Outwardly, Rachel took no more notice of Mardy than of the other children. But Mardy was sure that Rachel both recognised her own dislike and heartily returned it. It was a secret between them – the kind of personal, wordless secret usually shared only by close friends.

Rachel, naturally, had not even glanced up when Mardy and Hal had made their entrance. What she could see in the playground outside was bound to be more interesting, even if it was only a pyramid of swept leaves being rained on. Her hair was black like Mardy's, but not well-brushed, and with a dusty look as if she had had to push through cobwebs to leave the house. Her clothes were dusty too, especially the hand-knitted cardigan she always wore, so small it barely covered her shoulders. But that face! Those dark eyes! Mardy was frightened by Rachel's eyes sometimes – by the things they were looking at, that Mardy could not see. Her face was long and solemn when she was left to herself and that was most of the time. Spoken to, she started like a hare.

Mardy fumed. It was an act, it had to be. Probably Rachel was thinking of her at that very moment.

And – at that very moment – Rachel turned in her seat and looked directly at Mardy. She put her finger to her lips, and shushed.

* * *

"Did you see?" Mardy asked Hal in French, half an hour later. "*As-tu vu*?"

"*Je ne comprends pas*," shrugged Hal.

"Blockhead!"

"Quiet, Mardy!" Mrs Mumm was listening in on her headphones.

"Did you see?" Mardy mouthed at Hal. "She must have heard me thinking about her. I always thought she could."

Hal, quite reasonably, was unconvinced. "Mind games. Don't let her get to you."

Mardy looked despairing. "You don't understand about Rachel at all."

"What's to understand? She keeps herself to herself, that's all. Or would if people let her."

This way Hal had of being ploddingly sensible about *everything* was more than Mardy could bear. She made a disgusted noise in French. And that, for the moment, was the end of it.

But even Hal had to admit that what happened next was no accident.

Mrs Mumm was checking last week's homework, which had been to memorise the months of the year and the days of the week. She went round the class, asking each pupil in turn. Slim, pretty Mrs Mumm was another one who made Mardy think about her perfect weight. She seemed almost too young to be a teacher and so demure that an angry word would probably make her burst into tears – though her pupils soon learned that with Mrs Mumm appearances could be deceptive. Mardy liked her classes, but thought her far too fond of the language laboratory. The headphones made Mardy's ears sting.

Mrs Mumm was talking to Rachel. It seemed that Rachel had asked a question about one of the days of the week.

"Gras means 'fat', literally," Mrs Mumm was saying. "So Mardi Gras is just the last day before Lent – the last day of feasting."

"Thank you," said Rachel. "Mardi Gras. Fat Tuesday. I get it."

"That's the literal translation, yes," Mrs Mumm agreed cautiously. "But Fat Tuesday isn't really a phrase in English, is it?"

"Not yet," said Rachel, in the same neutral voice she had used throughout. She hadn't emphasised the words, not in the least. But then she hadn't needed to.

By lunchtime Mardy simply *was* Fat Tuesday. It was the Bluecoat girls who took to it most enthusiastically. Rachel did not need to say anything. She had lit the touchpaper; now she could stand back and watch.

"Pass the ruler, Fat Tuesday!"

"Shouldn't you be in the salad queue, Fat Tuesday?"

"Need some help squeezing through the fire doors, Mardi Gras?"

Mardy was glad to get to the end of the day. All the same, the prospect of visiting Alan was beginning to send a series of nervous shivers through her mind.

She dawdled, going home. As she reached the park she heard again the strange plucked instrument she had noticed on the way to school that morning. It was this, as much as a wish to drag out the time, that led her through the wrought-iron gates and up one of three forking paths, to a circle of flowerbeds and asphalt. The Undesirables were nowhere to be seen. In the middle of the circle stood a granite cross. Steps led up all around the cross, and on the side visible to Mardy a bunch of winter roses had been laid. *Lest we forget.* She began to read a dizzying list of names, each belonging to a dead soldier. Terence Appleby, William Aston, George Aston, Charles Ayling... Once she had begun, in fact, she found she had to carry on. The music, which was very close now – just on the far side of the cross – seemed to insist upon it. *Lest we forget.* She could not move further until she had dutifully read and remembered the name of each Burgess, Butterell, Chandler and Crisp; and so to the next side of the cross, and the next, until John Zipes had at last been laid to rest. And still there was no sign of where the music was coming from, or who was playing it.

Even now she could not move away. Mardy had heard that just before death a person's life flashed past – all in a moment. What happened to her now was like that, but much slower. She was unwillingly engaged in a laborious act of memory, unwinding each moment of her past like thread from a bobbin. She felt as if she had to or be turned to stone herself.

Finally – finally – the many-stringed instrument (a harp, was it, or a mandolin?) began drawing its threads of sound together. The tangle of arpeggios became more dense and knotted. Harmonies and discords vied dangerously, and at last a vast, enmeshed chord threw a net of closely-woven sound over her head. It billowed out and settled, dissolved at its edges and tightened at its centre, and bound her hand and foot.

For a few moments she was no more alive than a wax doll.

Then the music was not there any more.

Mardy gasped, as if she had just broken the surface after a long, lung-bursting swim. She was panting. About fifty yards away, at the far end of one of the paths, a dark figure carrying a black instrument case was leaving the park. The musician – if it *was* the musician – must have stopped playing some time ago, to have packed up and be leaving already. But that final, calamitous chord was still shaking Mardy, body and soul. It seemed only a few minutes since she had entered the park and seen the granite memorial. Since the music stopped it had been no time at all. Yet her watch told her that an hour had passed.

The hospital! Her mother had been expecting her home thirty minutes ago! Mardy ran up the path and the short streets to her own house. She was there in less than five minutes. Her mother's car was still parked in the road and the door was on the latch.

"Mum?" gasped Mardy breathlessly to the empty hall.

Mrs Watt was sitting on the living room sofa. Her visiting bag was beside her. She didn't look up. "Haven't you changed yet?" she asked coldly.

Mardy was too flustered to notice the oddness of this question. She plunged on with the excuse she had hastily prepared. "Sorry, Mum, I got held up at school.

Mr Lorimer wanted to talk about the rehearsals." She added quickly: "Hadn't we better get to the hospital?"

Mrs Watt stood up. She was a tall woman and she towered over Mardy now. "I don't know what you're babbling about, Mardy. Rehearsals? What are you sorry about?"

"About being late from school. A little bit late."

Mrs Watt shook her head. "I worry about you, Mardy, I really do. It was a good half hour ago you clattered up to your room to change. My only question is why you're *still* in your school uniform. Well, there's no time now. You'll have to go to the hospital as you are."

"Half an hour ago?" repeated Mardy, dumbfounded.

"At least. Now please get in the car. I don't like to keep Alan waiting. Do think about someone other than yourself for a change." Mrs Watt reached for her keys and purse. "Mardy! What are you doing *now?*"

"Just a moment!" yelled Mardy as she ran upstairs. She flung her school bag down on the landing and then stopped. She still had not got her breath back after her dash from the park. But something her mother had said was alarming enough for her to need to go to her room at once, even if it meant a shouting match later.

She had not gone upstairs half an hour ago. So who had?

Mardy opened the door of her room. Perhaps her mother was simply mistaken. But her mother did not often make mistakes – and there was something odd about this day which had made her nervous. That final chord from the War Memorial was still quivering through her.

But – no. The room was empty, and as familiar as her own skin. She would have felt at once if an intruder had been hiding there. She knew every stuffed toy and CD box and pile of unwashed clothes in the place, and not a stitch of it had moved since she had left the house that morning.

On her desk lay her page-a-day diary. She kept it only occasionally. Daily life already seemed wearing enough: why fire herself out twice by writing it down? But sometimes she felt she would overflow if she couldn't let out some of the things she couldn't even tell Hal. Some of these were about Alan – especially just before Christmas when he seemed to have had a relapse and was terribly close to death again. That had been a long, dark festival. But in the last weeks most of the entries had been to do with Rachel. On the page that lay open was a single jagged sentence, obviously written in a hurry:

Rachel Fludd is a witch!

Mardy stared at it hard and wrinkled her nose.

"Mardy!" Mrs Watt was calling from the hall downstairs.

"Coming, Mum!"

Mardy gave one last glance round her room.

Everything was as it should be. Everything was in its place... Except for that last sentence.

Rachel Fludd a witch? It was a suspicion she had often entertained, half seriously. It was certainly the kind of thing she might have put in her diary.

But, try as she might, Mardy could not remember writing it there.

2 LOVE POETRY

"WHY DON'T YOU tell me what's wrong?" asked Hal at last. They were nearing the end of Bellevue Road and Hobson's was just in view. Mardy was already fiddling unconsciously with her purse.

"Uh?"

"Mardy, wake up! Have you heard a word I've been saying?" Hal did a little war dance in front of her. What he had been saying was not important – a mixture of football, geography and soap opera – but Mardy usually made a better show of listening than this. "Is your brother worse again?" he finally asked outright.

"Alan? No, no. I saw him last night and he's just the same. A bit better if anything."

"I'm glad."

"His skin – you know it had that awful waxy look? Like a Granny Smith when you've polished it? That's gone. He doesn't look like he's wearing a mask any more."

Mardy relapsed into silence.

"But?" prompted Hal. "Come on, you know I can tell when something's bothering you."

"Only my mother's got this way of talking like he was a saint. And he isn't."

Alan wasn't a saint. Mardy loved her brother, but however much she tried to be pure and charitable, globules of resentment kept bubbling up through her mind whenever she thought about him, like marsh gas through a swamp. Little things, mostly, like the way he insisted on calling her Spud when he knew she detested the name. Or his habit of careless elegance which meant that, even lying motionless in his hospital bed, Alan was always the centre of attention. While their mother read Alan stories from the local paper, Mardy lurked in the background, picking off the less-wrinkled grapes for the man in the next-door bed and feeling like an imposter. She wished she could be filled with noble feelings, feelings of self-sacrifice and pity; instead, she wanted nothing more than to run back down the sterile corridors to her home.

They turned the corner to Hobson's. Mardy looked with naked dislike at the camera mounted on the school gate, which they were obliged to pass. Cameras gave her the creeps and the hospital was full of them.

"Hal – would you think I was crazy if I said I thought I was being followed?"

"*Followed!*" repeated Hal, instinctively looking back down the tree-lined road. "Who do you think's following you?"

"Don't say it like that – like you think I really *was* crazy! Anyway, I don't mean followed, quite. But watched. I think someone might be watching me."

"Mr Shute through the CCTV?" suggested Hal. "It's three minutes to nine again, we've got to hurry."

Mardy looked annoyed. "You don't understand," she said. "Wait while I go to Hobson's – I'll tell you after."

Mardy sprinted the fifty yards to Hobson's, rather flustered. She really had meant to tell Hal what was bothering her, but found it was not so easy to explain. Rachel Fludd came into it, and the diary entry, and the strange thing that had happened at the War Memorial the previous afternoon.

And Alan? Perhaps, thought Mardy furiously, perhaps everything comes into it. Perhaps it's another way of saying that life is strange, that the sky is blue and water is wet. A way of saying not much. But I'm not the kind of person who gets in a state over nothing, she thought. I'm just not that imaginative.

Mardy burst into Hobson's, steaming with frustration. Nut Krunch Bars, at least, were reliable.

Mrs Hobson looked up from her paper. "Oh. Hello, Mardy." For some reason she seemed surprised to see her. "What can I do for you?"

"My usual Nut Krunch," said Mardy. "I've finished with low-calorie imitations – they taste like cardboard. Back to double chocolate from now on."

Again Mrs Hobson looked at her oddly. "Back with a vengeance, I'd say. Two in half an hour is pushing it, isn't it?"

"What?" asked Mardy distractedly, as she placed the right coins on to the counter.

"Two Nut Krunch Bars in one day. You only just left the shop."

"What did you say?"

"Oh, not that it's any business of mine," protested Mrs Hobson. "I *know* what it's like, Fighting Temptation. Would you believe I used to have a twenty-six inch waist?"

"I haven't been in here since yesterday," protested Mardy.

"If you say so," laughed Mrs Hobson in an infuriating, disbelieving way.

"But I haven't!"

"Then all I can say is, your doppelganger was here ten minutes ago – and she likes double-chocolate Nut Krunch Bars too. Now, hadn't you better get along? Your friend's getting in a bit of a state out there."

True enough, Hal was standing at the window between two pyramids of baked beans, frantically tapping his watch. Mardy muttered a goodbye and left.

"Don't forget your chocolate!" called Mrs Hobson.

Another dash for the classroom. This time they almost ran into the school caretaker, Mr Bartok, who was screwing a bracket into the wall over the main entrance. "Mind my ladder!" he warned and teetered bulkily at the top.

Since Christmas the school had sprouted a ring of CCTV cameras. To keep out Undesirables, Mrs Watt had said, and a good thing too. But when Mardy saw Mr Shute, the headteacher, looking out over the playground from his first-floor office, she wondered. Perhaps it was the pupils, rather than any intruder, who were his main concern. She did not think she had ever been nearer to Mr Shute than the thirty feet separating them at the weekly assemblies, where he swept in, exhorted them and left. For all she knew Mr Shute might be a robot, or a hologram, or – or – anything...

Throughout assembly, Mardy kept looking up and down the hall, wondering who, if anyone, might have been mistaken for her. Perhaps, as Mrs Hobson had said, she really did have a double – or something close enough to fool the shopkeeper, who was shortsighted and always had her nose in the paper. Rows and rows of children surrounded her, short, tall, thin and fat, white, black and brown. From awkward Year 7s like herself to the willowy grandeur of Year 13, hundreds of girls in that room wore the Bellevue School sweatshirt. On hundreds of chests the same school logo was embroidered: a ship in full sail that actually looked more like a kitten being run over by a milk float.

Mardy couldn't decide which struck her more: how

very different everyone was or (in another way) how very much the same. They were all standing with their bored assembly expressions, as the head ran through arrangements for the Year 8 trip to the Science Museum. The same expressions persisted as he launched into the statutory hymn and warned them about the litter problem in the streets outside the school. But none of them, Mardy decided, looked enough like her to deceive Mrs Hobson.

Except, possibly, Rachel. But even Rachel was so much thinner, with her long blanched, moon face and coal-black eyes, that Mrs Hobson would have had to be blind not to see the difference. Rachel Fludd probably hadn't eaten a Nut Krunch Bar in her life.

It might not have been so bad if Rachel hadn't been writing in her notebook again at wet play that day. The children were kept in their classrooms, bored and out of temper. In the corner of Mardy's class Mrs Yarrow sipped away at a mug of coffee, clearly wishing she could be in the staffroom instead. Hal and his chess-playing friends found a set and retired to the corner. The room was as sweaty as a boxer's sock. Mardy, swinging her legs idly as she sat on the edge of a table, found without surprise that she and Rachel were the only two girls who had not attached themselves to some group or other.

Looking down at her own legs, she compared them with Rachel's. Fat Tuesday. String Bean Sally. Rachel must be as far under the perfect weight as Mardy was above it. There must be some perfect girl of whom they were both just freakish reflections. Certainly, something seemed to tie the two of them together. In the weeks since Rachel's arrival they had hardly ever spoken; yet Rachel seemed to fill a bigger place in her life than anyone else except Hal and her own family.

The battered leather notebook in which Rachel was writing was much less plush than the diary Mardy kept at home, but even that seemed another unwelcome link between them. And how furtively Rachel wrote! As if she were an enemy spy...

Despite herself, Mardy was curious to know what so absorbed Rachel. She got down from the table and made her way to Rachel's desk – not directly but by a route as aimless as possible. First, she stopped to check Hal's progress on the chessboard: he had just castled and was preparing to do something devastating with his rook. His eyes for once were narrowed, his lip bitten white with controlled ferocity. Mardy moved on, exchanging pleasantries with Kylie and Susannah at the expense of their friend Michelle, who was off that day with a cold. And so (under the flickering eye of Mrs Yarrow, who was probably itching for a cigarette) she arrived just behind Rachel. Rachel had not seen her approach or she would certainly have put the notebook into her pocket at once. Even so, Mardy could not see what she was writing because

Rachel had crooked her arm round protectively and she hung her head low over the paper with her hair falling raggedly around it.

So Mardy took a long shot.

"Who is he, then, Rachel?" she asked out loud. "Who are you writing love poems to?"

Rachel twisted round in alarm, blushed and hurriedly shut the notebook. A moment later it was not there – though Mardy didn't quite see which pocket she had put it in. All this happened in an instant, during which Mardy found herself backing off from Rachel's desk as though a hand had pushed her roughly away.

"Keep your nose out of it, Mardi Gras!"

Mardy staggered back to her seat. She was breathless and a little frightened at the fury she had managed to provoke in quiet, unobtrusive Rachel. But she was smiling too, because she had won some kind of victory. For Rachel to be made angry, she must have been touched at last. And Rachel did not like to be touched.

It didn't take long for the news that Rachel was in love to spread to the Bluecoat girls. The rest of the morning Mardy watched them prodding her like a spider in a jar. English, where they were reading *Romeo and Juliet*, presented almost too many opportunities to be true. Biology was just as good. Rachel had to wait until the maths lesson after lunch for the teasing to die down. Even then, the mystery of Rachel's boyfriend threatened to break out in unpredictable ways: an equation here, a co-ordinate there.

"And who are *you* co-ordinating with, Rachel?"

Mardy said nothing. She knew from her days as Queen of Fairlawn Primary just how little work was needed to start a rumour. Once the process was begun, any class would unite in the chase. Beyond Rachel herself, no one would suspect that Mardy was behind it at all.

Except Hal, of course. "Up to your old tricks, Mardy?" he said to her as they made their way down the corridor after maths. They were being buffeted like channel swimmers in a rough sea and it was with difficulty that Mardy managed to toss her head disdainfully and say: "I don't know what you mean."

"I'm sure you don't," said Hal, with his terrier face on. "I'm your friend, remember? I know the way you work."

"Oh shut up, Jiminy Cricket! When I need a conscience I'll advertise."

"You've got one already," retorted Hal between buffets. "Remember Theresa Greystoke?"

"Oh, her!" Buffet. Buffet. "I just felt sorry for the little squirt."

Mardy shifted herself so that she was separated from Hal beyond talking distance. She didn't care to be reminded of Theresa Greystoke.

For a brief time Theresa had been Mardy's rival at Fairlawn Primary. Beautiful, clever, an expert juggler and the owner of two ponies, Theresa had arrived from the north in her last year. For a while she had charmed everyone and Mardy had felt her own star beginning to lose some of its glitter.

But then a rumour started – and no one knew how – that Theresa Greystoke had had plastic surgery on her nose and ears. That those dazzling white teeth were dentures. That one of her bright blue eyes was actually made of glass. It was whispered too that Theresa Greystoke's father had bribed the headteacher to get good test results. Overnight, and without realising what had happened to her, popular Theresa Greystoke became an outcast.

Very little of this had come from Mardy directly. She had started the first rumour – only half expecting to be believed – then watched, in growing wonder, as the torrent had swept her rival from sight. In the end, she had rescued her. "Theresa Greystoke is my friend!" she had announced fiercely in the girls' toilets, where a Year 5 was scribbling something foul on the wall. It was enough. The word went out that Theresa was under Mardy's protection: the persecution ceased. Theresa herself – poor, trusting Theresa – had been terribly grateful.

Only Hal knew the whole story. Not that Mardy had ever told him, but he kept his eyes open, Hal did, and he understood Mardy too well for comfort. Mardy thought it over. So Hal thought that Rachel might become another

Theresa Greystoke, did he? If Mardy had still been Queen Bee, then yes – maybe. But Rachel and she were on equal terms here. The rest of the class thought little enough of either of them. That made it a fair fight, didn't it? And it was Rachel who had started it. Mardi Gras!

The next lesson was chemistry. Outside, the sleet had turned stutteringly to snow. At first the flakes were too large to settle, falling flat on their watery faces. But a little later there was a mother-of-pearl sheen to the asphalt and on the larch tree the small twigs hung exhausted under the weight of newly-gathered ice. In thirty minutes the playground was choked with it. Silent snow. The more Mardy looked at it the more she felt that it wasn't quite real, that the whole day had got off on the wrong foot and had better retrace its steps. She tried to concentrate on the test tube in front of her, on the blue flame from the Bunsen burner. In the distance – too distant to be made out clearly – there was a thin, whining hum. And *plink* – a sound like a string snapping or being plucked – and another... Water thawing and falling into pools of ice, ice breaking under its own weight and hunkering down into itself. And the burner's furnace flame roaring...

"Ouch!"

Two rows in front of her, Rachel jumped back in her seat as a tightly-folded wad of paper bounced stingingly off her cheek. Mardy didn't see who had thrown it. It must have flown past her own shoulder from somewhere at the back of the classroom. But from the way Rachel looked round as she bent to retrieve the paper it was clear whom *she* thought to blame. At her side, Hal too was peering at Mardy strangely: as if he hardly recognised her.

Rachel unfolded the paper. It was a piece of lined A4, just like the paper on a dozen pads all around the class. Just like the pad on Mardy's own desk. As Rachel read what was written there, Mardy saw her face flush darker with embarrassment and anger. She really seemed to be on the point of tears. When she looked round again it was with an expression of such shame and such knowledge, such open *dislike* – that it was Mardy who turned away.

"Whatever did you write on that note?" hissed Hal.

"Nothing! I mean – it wasn't me who threw it."

"No?" replied Hal with frank disbelief.

"No!"

Hal crooked a smile and peered at her again with that look of strange half-recognition. "Have it your way."

This made Mardy furious. "Why don't you believe me? Friends should trust each other!"

For the rest of the afternoon Hal made himself very busy with chemistry notes. When the final bell rang, Mardy waited for him at their usual spot, under the larch tree in the front playground. The snow had stopped falling, had thawed a little and then frozen harder, so that the asphalt was growing a treacherous, invisible skin, with an inch or so of snow underfoot. She saw Hal at an upstairs window once, being hustled along by a group of larger boys. Five minutes later she spotted his back, already halfway down the road from school. That was odd – he must have passed right by her. Even if he wasn't talking to her, how had she missed him?

Crunch crunch, like walkers on a gravel beach, the children left the school. Cars were waiting for many of them, lights on, moving tenderly up the road edges and away. Mardy hung back. She sketched a circle round the larch tree with her heel. She had not seen Rachel leave either and was thankful.

AT LENGTH, MARDY sighed and started up the long avenue of plane trees to the main road and the tangled streets beyond, one of which was her own. Already, the road had largely cleared. There were only a few children in sight. Some were trying to make snowballs from a fall no more than a fingernail's depth. The distracting snow suited Mardy. She did not want to talk to anyone. Now she had another incident to ponder and for once she did not miss Hal's company. Hal would have irritated her by telling her that her imagination was playing tricks. But Mardy suspected that a ghost had preceded her home yesterday and bought a Nut Krunch Bar from Mrs Hobson this morning. Perhaps the same ghost had been responsible for hitting Rachel with a piece of crumpled-up paper this afternoon. It was possible, she supposed. Mardy had heard of such things: poltergeists, they were called.

She had heard of other things, too. People fooling themselves, for a start. If you disliked someone the way she disliked Rachel, perhaps you might chuck something at her and then deny it – even to yourself. No one wants to think of herself as a bully, do they? And no one wants to think of herself as the kind of greedy pig who would scoff two Nut Krunch Bars in half an hour. How much easier to blame it all on a poltergeist, a double, an imposter...

By this time she was more than halfway up Bellevue Road, and nearly at Hal's house. Perhaps she *would* call on him after all. She could use some of his common sense now. Hal would keep her feet on the ground, frozen toes and all.

But there in front of Hal's front gate was a most unlikely group. Rachel Fludd herself was nearest, with her back to the street – and either side of her stood two of the Bluecoat girls, leering unpleasantly down the road at Mardy as if she had turned up on the underside of a shoe. They weren't just standing, either – they were standing *guard*: feet apart and waiting (Mardy was immediately certain of it) for Mardy herself. And from one of them came yesterday's catcall: "Mardi Gras!"

That was just the opening round. Most of it came from the Bluecoat girls, but not all. Mardy was surrounded by voices. The leaden clouds themselves were echoing back their low opinion of her.

"Lardy Mardy!"

"Pink and sweaty, legs like a Yeti, hair like a plate of cold spaghetti..."

"Where do you get your clothes from, Mardy? A tent-hire shop?"

"And who are you calling a witch?"

The last voice cut through the rest and silenced them. It silenced everything. Mardy could not help looking towards it. There was Rachel, standing alone. Gone were the Bluecoat girls, gone Rachel's own tearful sulk. Her dark eyes were trained on Mardy like shotgun barrels.

"Never," said Rachel, in a voice as cold as flint, "do that again. Ever."

She stepped into the road and began to cross without once taking her eyes off Mardy. Mardy realised with a jolt that Bellevue Road was not merely growing emptier as the school traffic cleared. It was quite deserted. The plane tree avenue stretched on into the distance and ended in a shimmer of sickly, yellow light that made her think of the smoke from damp leaves. It was the same both ways. No school any more, no shops, no people. Just two interminable rows of blinkered houses. Just Mardy and Rachel.

"Where is everyone?" Mardy asked, her voice trembling, as Rachel approached her. "What have you done?"

Rachel seemed different now, as everything was different: taller, more powerful. She did not speak at first. She was staring into Mardy's face, apparently searching there for some concealed mark or sign.

"Stand still!" she commanded – but distractedly, as if Mardy were a needle she was trying to thread, rather than a human being.

"Rachel, what's going on?" said Mardy.

"It must be here. Is it at the nape of your neck?"

"What?"

"Or inside your elbow? I'd have seen if it was in one of the obvious places."

"Rachel, listen to me! I don't know what you're talking about!"

"I'm looking for your mark, of course! The Crescent of Initiation! How else could you know I was a witch?" asked Rachel irritably. "How could you know a thing like that without being one yourself?"

"Are you crazy?"

"You wrote that note, didn't you? In the hieratic script! Foolish, foolish."

"I don't know what you're-'

"*And*, if more proof were needed," Rachel added in deep disgust, "here you are in Uraniborg itself." She gestured around her, to the smoky, yellow horizons at either end of the endless street and at the blank-eyed windows facing them.

Uraniborg. The word was strange to Mardy, but it seemed to waft through her mind like mist through moonlight, with a dreadful melancholy. She repeated, limply, that she wasn't a witch and hadn't called Rachel a witch – didn't even believe in witches (Rachel snorted here) and had certainly never heard of Uraniborg. "I just want to get home," she said.

Rachel did not seem to be listening anyway. Whatever she had been looking for on Mardy's face was obviously not to be found. Finally, she put her hands on her hips and admitted defeat.

"OK – I was wrong. You've got Artemisian blood, of course, but you're not an initiate."

She still seemed to be talking to herself more than to Mardy. Standing there in her school uniform – one size too small – with her face screwed up as if she was in the middle of a tricky maths problem, Rachel looked for a moment as out of place as Mardy felt. She wasn't at all Mardy's idea of a witch. But for all that, Mardy did not doubt her. Whatever else the air of Uraniborg did, it made believing that kind of thing easier.

Perhaps Mardy's eyes were only now growing accustomed to the strange light here; or perhaps it had only now chosen to show itself, but something was becoming visible at the end of the street – just where Bellevue School ought to have been. It was a tall, thick tower with a conical roof. Its walls, as far as Mardy could make out, were of rusty, red brick, but its roof was gold and in this sunless world it was the brightest thing she could see. Powered by some unseen engine, the roof was turning slowly and in complete silence. The golden tiles were revolving on the axis of that central turret.

Just coming into view was a place where the

expanse of gold was broken by a small square of darkness. Mardy realised that this was a raised hatch: one of the golden tiles had been lifted on a hinge and propped open. And from the hatch a tube projected, crimson and silver.

"A telescope?" said Mardy.

"The Mayor..." breathed Rachel. "Quick, I'll hide us."

There was a new and urgent note in her voice. Rachel began rubbing her hands together, one over the other, as if she were washing with soap. Within moments her hands were no longer empty. They held an object the size and shape of a duck egg, a smooth bolus of yellow smoke. She threw it to the ground, where it cracked open and bubbled out a dull, tarry liquid. Steam rose, the same nicotine yellow as the air of Uraniborg, and hung in a thick curtain between them and the tower. The tower was invisible again.

"If he's really looking hard for you, this won't stop him, of course," said Rachel. Even her voice was muffled by the curtain of yellow air. "Let's hope it's a routine survey."

Clearly, she expected Mardy to understand what she was talking about. But Mardy's incomprehension must have been obvious from her face.

"You really don't know what's going on, do you?" said Rachel.

"No. And I don't think I want to."

"I keep forgetting. It's because you've found your way here even though you don't understand about having a separable soul, and I don't see you how could have... Oh, *bother!*"

Rachel looked petulant, as if she had failed to guess a simple riddle. She even stamped her foot. "Oh, bother!" she repeated. "I see it all now."

She stood there biting her lip for such a long time that Mardy was eventually forced to prompt her: "What do you see?"

"What you're here for, of course! We knew he was preparing the Binding Spell again, but I never thought he'd act so fast. Come to the horse trough and I'll show you."

Rachel took Mardy's hand and turned about so that they were facing the blank wall between Hal's house and the next. Only now the wall was no longer blank. Most of the pavement was obscured by a large stone trough and above it a tombstone-shaped plaque had been engraved in leafy letters.

Weary traveller take your ease
Lay down the burden that you carry,
It is compact of foolish cares
Then stay and by this fountain tarry.
Life's a race not won by hurry
Chasing every flattering breeze
Let Fortune brag and Care be sorry
Weary traveller take your ease.

Near the bottom of the plaque a cherub puffed his cheeks and blew. A green copper pipe projected from his mouth like a pea-shooter and there was a pump handle.

"Don't look so surprised," said Rachel. "It's been there all the time, you know."

Mardy was quite certain that it had not, but she did not wish to provoke another of Rachel's snorts by protesting. She noticed, however, as she and Rachel moved the few paces to the horse trough, that the curtain of yellow air Rachel had created followed them obediently, smudging the light as it came and blocking the far end of the street from view.

The trough was empty, but Rachel began working the pump at once. At first, she produced nothing but a hollow clanking, alarmingly loud in the empty street. Then the clank got mixed up with a deep-throated gargle, the gargle progressed into a gloop and finally a stream of rather murky water spilled from the pipe. Filling the trough took some time, but long before Rachel had stopped pumping it was obvious that water in Uraniborg was not what Mardy was used to. As it rippled and spun at the bottom of the trough, mixing with dust and moss and fragments of twig, it also found time to glisten. It was thicker than ordinary water, with a metallic look to its surface, and somehow sluggish. What was strangest, amidst the scum and bubbles Mardy sometimes thought she caught a reflection of people or places quite unknown to her. A circle of women chanting in a forest clearing. The inside of a bedouin tent. A venerable Chinese face, frowning intently and just on the point of speech. Then the water would eddy and slide to a new angle.

"That should be enough," said Rachel at last. She sounded out of breath from all that pumping. She stood beside Mardy, waiting for the water to settle. In her hand was a pin. When the water was still, she took Mardy's finger quickly and

"Ouch!"

"Don't be a baby. I only need a drop."

Rachel had pricked the very tip of Mardy's index finger. Now she was holding the finger over the trough, squeezing out a cherry-red bead of blood. Mardy seemed unable to do anything but submit and watch as if it were all happening to another person – though the pain in her finger was sharp enough.

"The pin's silver – the only substance that will pass freely between the Mayor's world and your own."

"It still hurts!"

"The blood will earth you," Rachel explained. "We must show the spirit the way to its lodging."

She let the pin fall. As it hit the water it ripped a hole in its surface, like a bullet tearing through cloth. Through the hole Mardy saw things moving. Very small things, it seemed – or perhaps just a long way down. She was looking at the world from the bottom of a cloud. She blinked.

"That's – *here!* Bellevue Road! I can see the trees, and people walking about in the snow, and—"

"Yes?"

"And me," Mardy added weakly. "Only it can't be..."

It was. Mardy saw herself plodding up the road from Hal's house, her shoulder bag swaying to left and right as she hugged herself against the cold.

"You *are* there," said Rachel. "In body, I mean. If one of your friends came along now and spoke to you, you'd smile and say hello and do all the things people do when they pass the time of day. And perhaps they'd never guess your immortal spirit was here in Uraniborg. Unless they looked into your eyes...'

"Just stop it!" shouted Mardy. "This is getting too weird for me. No one can be in two places at once."

"Calm yourself," said Rachel soothingly, and she laid a hand gently on Mardy's arm. Perhaps she was trying to be kind, but Mardy knew that part of Rachel was enjoying herself thoroughly. Rachel could not quite keep a sneer out of her voice as she added: "Whoever said Uraniborg was a *place*? It's a way of being, that's all. A way of living in spirit."

"It *looks* like a place."

"Because you're used to three dimensions," said Rachel condescendingly, as if that were a common shortcoming. "You see it all that way, of course. You don't know any better."

"But whatever it is, I still don't know why I'm here.

Maybe you like it – if you're a witch like you say."

"Like you *wrote*!"

"I did not – I've told you! And what's more," Mardy added quickly, seeing Rachel about to interrupt again, "I don't know anything about witches, and I've never seen a ghost, and I think Halloween is an advertising racket. I don't like adventures, understand? And I've had enough of you treating me like some puzzle you've got to solve, Rachel Fludd."

"Shh! Don't say my name out loud. The Mayor's got ears as well as eyes. Sharp, sharp!"

"There's no need to twist my hand! I promise I won't say your precious name again. Just tell me what's happening."

Rachel gave her a long, hard look. "It's quite simple. It's the Mayor. He wants your soul, to slave for him up there." She gestured cautiously through the air-curtain, towards the tower behind it. "And if you're already visiting Uraniborg, he's well on his way to getting it."

"Who's this Mayor you keep talking about?" demanded Mardy. The bit about slaves sounded too alarming. "Is he Count Frankenstein or something?"

"You don't think I know his name, do you?" exclaimed Rachel. "He's – well, he's a very strong enchanter, that's all. He's old, you see, and clever, and he knows all the Harmonic Combinations – he's had a long time to learn them. Spells of binding and releasing, summoning and breaking – he probably knows more about them than anyone except the Artemisians themselves. And he's got hundreds of spirits waiting on him and spying for him. There's no hiding for long." She added, a little resentfully: "He doesn't like us Artemisians at all."

"I see," said Mardy, who didn't, of course – but just now she couldn't think of anything else to say. Except the most important thing and it took her a little time to summon the nerve to ask it. "These slaves. How does he get them?"

"By calculating their Reverberant Chord, usually. Everyone has one – unique, like a fingerprint – but it needs a great enchanter to work it out. Have you heard any strange music recently?" Rachel asked in a serious and methodical way. "String music – strings being plucked?"

Mardy thought immediately of the War Memorial and the thought-deadening music she had heard there. How it had seemed to pluck at *her* and shake the soul out of her body like a coin out of a piggy bank. "Yesterday – after school. I think I may have seen the Mayor, too."

"His face?" asked Rachel excitedly.

"Just the back of him, as he was walking away. He had some kind of instrument in a case. Anyway, since then – things have happened to me. Odd things..."

Mardy told Rachel about her conversation with Mrs

Hobson that morning and the intruder in her room. "I keep thinking I've got a double following me about."

Rachel nodded. "That's likely enough. A Fetch. Like the one we just saw. It's a copy of you, made when the Mayor played the Reverberant Chord. Right now he'll be nursing it up, getting it ready to take your place."

"Take my place?" echoed Mardy.

"That's the idea. You wane, it waxes. It's not a straightforward process, mind. You'll probably find it fades in and out for a while. But make no mistake, in the end the Fetch will *be* Mardy Watt and you'll be a slave for ever here in Uraniborg. And none of your friends or family will know that anything's changed."

"Of course they will!" protested Mardy. "Do you think they wouldn't notice the difference between me and a Fitch?"

"That's 'Fetch'," corrected Rachel. "Oh, I don't say they won't see any change at all. 'Mardy's in a strange mood today,' they'll say. 'She's just not herself. And hasn't she gone off her food? I hope she's not sickening for something.'"

Rachel did her impression in a high, adenoidal voice, which made Mardy furious. She's not even taking it seriously! she thought.

"The copy's never perfect – but it'll probably be good enough while it's needed."

Mardy sensed some hope in this. "So the Fetch won't take my place for ever?"

"How could it? It's not a real person, you know. More like a very clever clockwork toy. And eventually it will run down. That's the way it works. Everyone thinks you're getting sick – and sicker. No one knows what's wrong. The doctors are baffled – nothing seems to help. A few days, a few weeks maybe, and it's all over. Your family thinks you're dead – but you're not. You're really up here, a slave for the Mayor. All that they bury is a body. But of course, you mustn't let it get to that stage."

Rachel paused, apparently unwilling to broach some unpleasant detail. Mardy asked reluctantly: "What do you mean?"

"Once the Fetch is dead, that's it. There's no way back. As far as the world's concerned, that's the end of you. Your soul will be stuck here for ever, here with the Mayor as your master. So you've got to act fast." Rachel thought for a moment. "Is this the first time you've seen Uraniborg?"

"Yes."

"Absolutely sure?"

"It's not something I'd forget!" exclaimed Mardy.

"And you'd never seen your Fetch before? Till just now, I mean?"

"Not till just now – no."

Rachel looked relieved. "Then the spell's not too far advanced. With luck. The best thing you can do—"

Rachel was about to say more, but something behind Mardy's back had caught her attention. Mardy turned –

to see a large, cumbersome vehicle coming down the street towards them. It was still some distance away, but Mardy could already see that it ran on caterpillar tracks like a tank. There did not seem to be anyone driving it. It was wide too – wide enough to fill the entire street. Slowly as it came, there was no escaping it.

"It's the street cleaner," said Rachel and she sounded more nervous than she had since Mardy had entered Uraniborg. "The Mayor must have spotted us. Prepare to get wet."

Mardy saw what Rachel meant. Fitted at intervals along the sides of this contraption were jets of water and big tumbling brushes like those in a car wash. Everything in the street was getting soaked. There was something so relentless about it that there seemed no point in even trying to run away. In fact, as the machine drew closer (and already it was surprisingly close), Mardy saw through the jets that the street itself was melting at the touch of water. Between her and the street cleaner lay Uraniborg, a smoky, yellow suburb of nowhere at all. Behind it, Bellevue Road itself was springing back into being: the school, snow-bound trees, Hal's parents' splash of colour. And now the machine was upon them. Rachel's smokescreen dispersed instantly as a spurt of water crashed into it.

At the last moment Rachel took Mardy's hand: "Just close your eyes and try not to make a noise," she hissed.

Then Mardy felt the water burst on to her and through her. It was worse than she could have imagined. She had expected to get wet and had been gritting her teeth for the feeling of ice-cold water on her skin. But she had not expected the water to jet right through her body, melting her lungs and heart and bones and brain, or to leave behind it (the last thing she noticed before her nose too disintegrated) such an oily, chemical smell. There was no pain. But the atomising fear was worse than any pain. "I'm a ghost!" thought Mardy. Then there was no Mardy any more and nothing more to be thought.

At least, not in Uraniborg. In Bellevue Road Mardy was catching her breath. She found herself near the park, leaning shakily against a wall. She looked down at her own hand, which only a moment before had been pocked with holes where water from the street cleaner had begun to spray her. Her clothes were not even damp, though there was still a cold, metallic feeling where the water had struck her tongue, as if she had spent the last half hour sucking an icicle.

Rachel was gone. A white transit van was driving slowly down the street, probably looking for a house number. In the time she had been in Uraniborg the snow had decided to thaw again and was already slushing in the gutter. She hurried to her own house and let herself in, shedding her coat and shoes in the front hall.

"Mum? You home?"

From beyond two closed doors her mother shouted a reply, but the words were impossible to make out. Mardy didn't mind. She had just wanted to make sure she wasn't alone in the house. Her mother might be hard to handle, but she was not the sort of person who would easily be whisked off to Uraniborg. She was far too solid for that.

Mardy was surprised – even shocked – to discover that she was hungry. In the kitchen she made herself a honey sandwich, being careful not to spread the butter too thick. Then a mug of hot chocolate to sip at in front of the television. *Style Squad* was doing a special today on 'Makeovers for your Pet' which sounded just right. She would sink into the largest beanbag, watch and try to forget about Uraniborg.

Holding her mug in one hand and her plate in the other she backed into the living room door. For some reason the door failed to slam back into wainscoting. Mardy had to push quite hard to open it wide enough to enter. She peered in to see what was causing the obstruction.

The room was hardly recognisable. Cushions and blankets were scattered across the floor; plates and mugs (including Mum's Jubilee mug that *no one* was allowed to touch) had been tipped over and hot chocolate was seeping into the new cream carpet. Next to the sofa lay discarded video boxes, tissues, magazines, half a dozen cushions from the sofa. The scene would not have looked particularly strange in Mardy's own room. But Mrs Watt's living room was always immaculate. It was one of her points of honour – and Mrs Watt was a very honourable woman. It had been tidy when Mardy had left for school that morning, she was sure of it.

So what – or who – had happened?

Mardy didn't get a chance to wonder for long. Her mother was standing just behind her.

"That's right," said Mrs Watt softly. It was her gentle voice, the one Mardy dreaded most. "Take a good, long look."

"It – it wasn't me, Mum," she began.

"Don't talk. Look," Mrs Watt suggested. She walked Mardy forward, not roughly but irresistibly. "Here – fifteen wrappers from your favourite sweets – that minty chewy concoction. And here (watch out for the orange peel, mind your feet) is where you've been writing on the back of Alan's armchair. 'Rachel Fludd stinks!' – a charming sentiment..."

"But I never—"

"Mardy, if you can't be bothered to hide the evidence, at least don't make it worse by lying about it. Who exactly am I meant to think was responsible? Did a burglar come and slob in front of the TV half the afternoon? Has the house been visited by sweet-toothed aliens?"

"It's not impossible..."

"Or has my daughter simply mistaken the living room for a doss-house? Well, Mardy? Well? *Look at me!*"

Mardy looked at her. The sequence was always the same with her mother. Quiet first, then sarcastic – and then there was a point where the sarcasm swelled like a toad's throat and out came a flood of anger no one could control. Mardy could only wait and hope it would go no further. But even as she groped for the right, calming words, questions were burning in her own head: *Who did this? And where are they now?*

At that moment, the floorboard above their heads creaked, just the way it did when Mardy walked from her bedroom door to her desk. She and her mother looked up at the same time, so it couldn't have been imagination.

"Did you hear that?" Mardy said quickly, sidestepping her mother and making a dash for the door. "There's someone upstairs."

"You will *not* run out of the room when I'm talking to you!" screamed Mrs Watt. "I won't have it!"

But Mardy had already gone – and she was shaking so much as she climbed the stairs that she had to grab the banister to keep from stumbling. The thought of what might be waiting in her bedroom frightened her, but her mother's voice did so no less. She had always been scared of that voice. It could hold her just as tightly as any magic dreamed up in Uraniborg, and cut as deeply too. But she had to see what was in her room...

The door was open. No lights were on, but even by the dim, snow-reflected glow of the street she perceived the outline of a girl sitting in the chair at her desk. She didn't recognise her at first. Mardy had never seen herself from behind. But the Fetch had undoubtedly heard her come in, for it turned slowly in the chair, placing its hands on its knees. With its grey, dead eyes, it was looking directly at her.

"Hello Mardy," it said with Mardy's voice. It smiled Mardy's smile, as if it were about to share a deep, delicious secret, just between the two of them. "I'm you."

4 LOSING WEIGHT

MARDY STARED. IT was herself. Perfect as a mirror's reflection. But where a mirror would have shown the horror now growing in her own face, the Fetch's expression did not falter. The Fetch laughed and shook its hair back over its shoulder, just as Mardy did forty times a day. And these actions, so familiar and instinctive as to be part of her, made it more alien than any stranger's face could be. Mardy screamed. She shut her eyes, opened her mouth and let the scream block everything: the Fetch in front of her, her mother coming up the stairs behind. It all became light-headed blindness, white noise, a tingling in her fingertips and toes, and then the relief of her own conscious mind buckling under these things and – gratefully – nothing at all.

The next thing she knew was a kind of insistent blinking in her mind. Flapping light and wind. She opened her eyes to find the room shaking itself like a wet dog, flinging droplets of colour everywhere – until finally it curled itself about her in its familiar shape.

Directly above her face a tube of pink light quivered slightly, then shrank back into the brittle outline of her mother's face.

"—hear me?" she was asking, but her voice was eerie and strange in Mardy's head.

"I think I'm going to be sick," said Mardy. Then she remembered the Fetch, and sat up too quickly to look at the chair where it had been sitting. The chair was empty.

"Did you see it?" she asked her mother, gripping her sleeve. "My double? It must have come past you."

"First things first," said Mrs Watt. "Have you hurt your head?"

"My head? No, I... don't think so."

"I don't think so either – there's no lump." Mrs Watt ran her fingers over Mardy's scalp. "If you're going to be sick, we'd better get you to the bathroom."

Mardy found that there is nothing like ten minutes spent kneeling over a lavatory bowl to put supernatural fears into perspective. Though she never stopped believing in what she had seen, it began to feel distant and less horrific. She wondered briefly whether she should confide in her mother – but the thought of Mrs Watt's face on hearing that her daughter had been bewitched was almost as frightening as the Fetch itself. Perhaps she could have told Alan, she thought – if Alan had been there to tell.

Mrs Watt slapped a cold flannel over her face. "So – what frightened you exactly?"

"It was the... I suppose it must have been a shadow."

"Shadow!" repeated Mrs Watt. But she did not press the matter. And that surprised Mardy, because "having things out" was something her mother usually insisted on, like rinsing the dishes or sweeping the crumbs off the tablecloth – it was a kind of spiritual housework. She wondered if her mother too had seen something in the late afternoon light that she would rather not discuss.

The Fetch seemed to be gone now, in any case.

That night did not pass easily. Mardy could not find a way of lying in her bed that let her see the whole room at once. To begin with, she wedged herself into the corner of her bottom bunk. She was anxious that there should be no chance of anyone coming at her from behind. But then she seemed to hear creaks, and even breathing, from the bunk above. She expected to find the Fetch's face – horribly inverted this time, with its hair hanging down – staring into hers. So she tried lying in the top bunk, only to find the creakings promptly transferred to the bed below. Besides, the writing desk where the Fetch had first appeared lay between her and the door. The books and ornaments beyond had a nasty trick of arranging themselves by the light of the street lamp (Mardy had left the curtains open a little) into the shapes of head, hair, elbows and glinty little eyes.

Finally, after she had heard her mother go to bed, she put her desk light on and read till daybreak.

* * *

When Mrs Watt entered Mardy's bedroom the next morning with the ritual cup of hot chocolate, she found Mardy sitting at her desk, fast asleep in her pyjamas. At any rate, that was what she saw in the end. At first, she thought the room was empty. It was a mess, of course. Mardy's bed sheets had been tossed like salad leaves, but her mother did not think they had actually been slept in. Through the half-drawn curtains there was an irritable flicker from the net curtain, itching at the glass. Mrs Watt's sense had been of entering an empty room: her first thought had been that Mardy must have absconded through the open window.

She looked again – more carefully this time – and even so had to blink and rub her eyes before she was able to recognise the hillock of shadow over by the desk as a human being. As Mardy.

"Mardy, what are you doing?"

Mrs Watt leaned over her daughter and pulled the curtain smartly back. The pattern of clouds and castles was a little young for her daughter now, of course. But these things cost money, so...

"Wake up, Mardy! It's seven o'clock."

"Uh?" Mardy's shoulders hunched. "Is it morning?"

"Of course! A school morning too."

Mardy groaned somewhere within her folded arms. She raised her head unwillingly to the light. Her face was lined where it had been pressed into the folds of her pyjamas, and her eyes were pink and sore. "I think I may have become nocturnal," she said. "Daylight doesn't suit me any more."

Mrs Watt was having none of that. "You've got clean underwear in the drawer. Breakfast in ten minutes sharp. Is your homework done?"

"Homework? Oh..."

"Geography and history on Wednesday. It's all on the calendar."

"They really don't mind if you're late once in a while. I've had such a weird night," Mardy began.

"Hmm." Mrs Watt automatically began tidying around her. "I don't know what's got into you, Mardy, this last couple of days. Has something happened at school?"

"No, no," said Mardy hastily. Which was almost true. Compared with the park and Bellevue Road, her time at school had been virtually normal. "I'm all right, Mum. I just didn't sleep well. A nightmare – you know."

Mrs Watt said nothing, but her expression shifted. She looked at Mardy directly again and in a new way. In a different voice she added: "You could take the morning off if you're not well. It's my half day."

Mardy sat up. "No. I'm fine, really."

"Sure?"

"Yes, Mum, don't fuss."

"I'm allowed to worry, aren't I?" complained Mrs Watt. "And if you're going down with something it's important to catch it early. I learned with Alan-'

Whatever she had been going to say was cut short by the slamming of the front door in the hall below. A moment later, footsteps were crunching down the path to the street.

The gate at the end of the path clanged twice. Once lightly and once with an emphatic rattle for luck. Only one person shut the gate like that.

"Mardy?" Mrs Watt began. They both moved to the window and peered into the pre-dawn darkness. Last night's snow still scabbed the hedge tops and the church roof opposite. The streetlights outside were yellowing the puddles. The pavement seemed deserted at first. Then Mardy saw the Fetch, already dressed in school uniform, heading in the direction of the park. Even in this light there was no mistaking it.

But Mrs Watt turned briskly from the window. "Must have been the wind, knocking the gate."

"But, Mum, didn't you see—"

"I see a girl who didn't get enough sleep last night," Mrs Watt replied quickly. "You're barely more than a shadow of yourself, Mardy. Let's get you in the shower."

Mardy *felt* barely more than a shadow as she stumbled to the bathroom – albeit a shadow with limbs as heavy as clay. But her mother was right: the shower did bring her back to life, and so did the grapefruit body scrub, the spearmint mouthwash, the cream for her toes that claimed to be made from seaweed and kiwi fruit. Either she was coming back to life, she thought, or she was being most pleasantly embalmed. If only she weren't so clumsy! The soap, and even the big loofah sponge, kept slipping from her grasp. Nor did she forget (though she managed for a time not to think about it) that look in her mother's eyes when she had denied seeing the Fetch. It wasn't a look Mardy had often seen on Mrs Watt. Her mother had been frightened.

Breakfast was a strange meal. The previous night was not mentioned. Her mother had restored the living room to a respectable condition, but there were none of her usual acid remarks about Mardy's slovenliness. That made Mardy surer still. Mrs Watt was avoiding the subject of the Fetch and any other subject likely to lead to it. Mardy registered the fact, but she was more concerned with other matters. Particularly where the Fetch was and what crimes it might even now be committing in the name of Mardy Watt. The mess in the living room had been unpleasant enough, but Mardy feared the Fetch would be capable of anything. Its eyes had not been human at all.

At the same time as she was worrying about the Fetch, a different part of her brain was trying to do ordinary things like spread butter and pour milk. But it was a frustrating business, for her clumsiness seemed to be getting worse. Knife handles slipped through fingers, plates clunked into cups and spilt tea on the crisp new cloth. If Mrs Watt hadn't been avoiding the subject of untidiness, there might have been another confrontation. As it was she just looked at Mardy strangely. "You're not really with us today, are you, Mardy?"

Mardy shook her head meekly.

"An early night tonight. No arguments."

Mardy did not feel like arguing. "I could sleep for ever."

Then Mrs Watt made more noises about keeping her off school – but that was the last thing Mardy wanted. She had to find the Fetch – and, even more, she had to find Rachel. Rachel was the only one who might be able to help. Mardy set off for school, only a little late. The park railings flicked past. The grass and bushes still wore a little bubbling skin of snow, but the thaw had done its work: the pavement was a patchwork of sludgy puddles. Mardy glanced at the sky. Grey and echoless it looked, with fold upon fold of heaped cloud. At the top of every third lamp-post she saw that a closed-circuit television camera had been mounted. They whirred occasionally. She had never noticed them before – but that didn't mean they had not been there. She was beginning to feel there were many things in this world – most of them unpleasant – whose existence she had never previously suspected. Unheard-of rules, too, for a game she had not known she'd been playing.

She rang Hal's doorbell. After the usual crashes and shouts of "I'll get it!" she heard the latch click and there stood Hal's mother, looking unexpectedly immaculate in a business suit. She must be going to a meeting, thought Mardy.

"Morning. Has Hal left for school yet?" Mardy asked as brightly as she could.

Mrs Young did not answer at first. She did not seem to have heard. She kept staring at a spot on the end of Mardy's nose. Or rather, Mardy thought, she was staring beyond her nose, beyond *her* – into the street behind. The look on her face was one of puzzlement and slight alarm.

"Hello?" said Mrs Young. "Who is it?"

"It's me, Mardy!" cried Mardy. Mrs Young's expression flickered a little, as if she had heard some small but troubling sound – the whine of a mosquito perhaps. She squinted again at the space where Mardy stood: but if she saw anything it was no more than a small vexation of the air, hazy with shadow.

Mardy realised with horror that to Mrs Young she was virtually invisible. Whatever spell had been put on her was growing stronger. And suddenly, rather than fear, she felt a rush of burning anger. How dare anyone do this to her! How dare anyone steal her life! She shouted at the top of her voice. "IT'S ME! I'M HERE – MARDY WATT! LOOK AT ME, CAN'T YOU?"

This time Mrs Young certainly reacted. She gave a start and rubbed her eyes. "Mardy?" she said, staring at Mardy as if at a mirage. She looked quite frightened.

"Yes, yes, I'm here!" replied Mardy, waving her arms. But even as she did so, the recognition faded from Mrs Young's face. She shook her head and muttered something about the folly of eating Gorgonzola after midnight. The door was shut.

Mardy gazed down at herself. She still seemed solid enough. Her shoe, planted firmly on the path, was letting in perfectly real water. But ghosts probably do think of themselves as real, she reflected. They probably think it's everything else that's ghostly. "I *am* me!" she said out loud. "I'll show them I am!"

Once more she reached for the doorbell and pressed. Her finger slid off to the side. She tried again, and again. Each time the doorbell refused to budge and her finger slipped across its surface like quicksilver. It was the same sensation of clumsiness that had come over her at breakfast. But now she saw that it was nothing to do with clumsiness after all. Her body was getting *thinner*. Not thinner like the girls she admired in *Fave!* magazine, but thinner like weak cocoa. She was dissolving, losing her power even to touch physical objects. Somehow it was more frightening than not being heard or seen. It made her feel more cut off from the world – a ghost indeed. How far would it go? Would she soon be unable to breathe so much as a mouthful of air? Her chest felt tight at the thought of it.

Mardy set off slowly up the road to school. There seemed nothing else to do. A little way along she saw a small twig lying on the pavement. She bent to pick it up. If she could, she decided, there was hope. If not...

She did not give that thought a chance to settle. Her fingers were already gripping the twig. She pulled. As soon as she did so she could feel it sliding through her hand, as slippery as a greased pig. She tried again, more carefully this time – but with the same result. She wanted to wail with frustration, but then felt strongly that she must not. If she did, he would see: and know that he was winning.

He?

Mardy had no idea where that word had come from. Then she realised that all the time she had been experimenting with the chestnut twig she had also been casting anxious looks back up the street to the CCTV cameras mounted on lamp-posts along the street. But those cameras belonged to the police, didn't they? Or some private security firm? Not to one person, anyway. All the same, the one she was looking at now seemed to blink at her haughtily behind its monocle of glass. All down the road to school the lamp-posts marched on and on, two rows of eyes on stalks. There seemed to be no end to them – no school either, but a harsh, stone, cylindrical building, from the roof of which a Watcher was certainly observing her through another thick, glass lens. She felt their eyes meet.

Then there was a strange kaleidoscopic twist to the light and the lens winked shut, leaving the street disenchanted. Mardy was surrounded by children walking up towards the school gates. The cream and concrete school buildings waited beyond. There were cameras mounted on some of the lamp-posts, but these too now seemed ordinary. They even had a name – SECURITECH – and a phone number printed on the side. It was as if someone had been creeping up on her and, when detected, had instantly fallen back to a safe distance.

"What's the time, Mr Wolf?" Mardy asked aloud.

She bent to pick up the twig. It came this time, easily enough – though there was still a slight rubberiness to her fingers she would have liked not to notice. She felt relieved: it was a victory, however small. But it was not a final one. The Mayor, or whoever was behind this, would not give up so easily. He was cautious, patient, an angler with all the time in the

world. He might have fallen back to a safe distance:
that did not mean he had given up the chase.

All the way to school Mardy was eyeing the children
around her and wondering: Can she see me? Can he?
Can they? Or am I invisible to everyone now? Certainly
no one paid her any attention, but that was not so
unusual, she realised. Most people are invisible, most
of the time. They hurry on, fogged with their own plans
and worries, and they don't see the strangeness all
around them. Perhaps the existence of Uraniborg
depends on that.

Meanwhile, only the cameras on the lamp-posts
seemed to acknowledge her. They whirred and jittered
whenever she made her way beneath them. And up ahead
in the school she felt another eye following her from an
upstairs window. Not a friendly eye, but greedy and
possessive. It never faltered. Was it the Mayor, somehow
seeping through from Uraniborg? Or was it someone in
the school itself who was studying her so relentlessly?

Mardy came to the playground just as the bell rang
for registration. Almost without thinking she joined the
migration of pupils toward the main entrance. She had
no plan. To do the usual thing seemed easiest. But
soon she felt herself being jostled more roughly than
normal.

"Steve! Wait up!"

A pair of Year 8 boys were pushing through the
crush to reach one of their friends. Mardy was in their

way. The larger of the boys lunged towards her – then abruptly pulled back, blinking. Judging by his face, Mardy knew that he had seen her – or seen *something*. His companion, a red-haired, thin-faced boy, was less cautious. His elbow crashed into her ribs and Mardy winced with the pain she knew must follow. But instead, she felt only a strange, itching irritation and a movement deep within her body, as though someone were trying to make balloon-animals from her intestines. She yelped and pushed the boy away – only to feel her hand slide over his sharp nose and forehead and bounce back over the springy coils of his red hair.

He must have felt something too then, for he drew back his arm at once and looked very oddly at the space where Mardy was standing. But a moment later the body-tide had carried him off into the school building.

Mardy waited until there was no one about, then padded down the noiseless corridors until she came to her own classroom. A window was set in the door and she looked inside. There was Mrs Yarrow, calling out the register. There were the Bluecoat girls. Over by the windows, Rachel's place was empty – which set a queasy feeling loose at the back of Mardy's stomach. Reluctantly, she shifted her gaze towards the back of the class, where she and Hal usually sat. Hal was leaning forward with his head between his hands, absorbed in a book. Mardy could not be sure, but he seemed to be pointedly ignoring the person at Mardy's own desk, as if they had had a row. That person, Mardy saw with a groan of recognition, was the Fetch. The Fetch was looking demure and attentive in Mardy's school uniform, clearly trying not to attract attention.

"Mardy Watt?" called Mrs Yarrow as she reached Mardy's name in the register.

"Here, Miss!" called the Fetch at once. Even through the classroom door it was obvious to Mardy that the person speaking was not her and could never be mistaken for her. She would never have sounded so prim and eager, so insufferably keen to get in Mrs Yarrow's good books. Mrs Yarrow would notice, surely. Everyone would notice now and realise that the creature sitting in her place was not Mardy Watt at all but a lumpen imitation.

To her horror, Mrs Yarrow looked at the Fetch and smiled in surprised approval. "Hal Young?" she continued.

Hal had cast a strange look at Mardy (No, thought Mardy, not at me, at the Fetch!) when it had called out. But he merely replied "Here" in his usual neutral tone, and Mrs Yarrow passed on.

Mardy could bear no more. She slid out of the building and waited till breaktime, watching Mr Bartok marshal the leaves into neat piles. Even here in the school playground there were CCTV cameras. She and Hal had seen Mr Bartok installing them just after Christmas. The headteacher had insisted on it, Mr Bartok had told them.

At half past ten a bell rang and the playground was suddenly swarming. Mardy found herself quite dizzied by the children as they ran and bickered, swung on branches, fought, whispered their own desperate secrets and shouted other people's, sulked, screamed and enjoyed themselves. It was an ordinary morning breaktime, but she was more easily shaken now. She felt vulnerable as she stood invisibly amidst this random frenzy. At last she saw Hal – on his own, thank goodness. She walked towards him, then stopped. Would Hal be able to see her? She hadn't even thought about it. Now she did, it seemed unlikely. But something about the way he sat scowling at the Fetch (which had just emerged into the playground, looking even sprucer and more righteous than before) gave her hope. She planted herself right in front of Hal and smiled.

"Hello, Hal."

Hal took his glasses off and squinted. He examined the lenses, as if to remove a gnat or a speck of dust. Then he looked back at her. "Mardy? Is that really you?"

"Of course it's me, you lunk-brained troll! Who else would it be?"

Hal clearly didn't like to say. But to Mardy's surprise he gave a low chuckle. "I knew she was a fake from the start!"

"You did?" cried Mardy with relief. "You saw through her?"

Hal nodded. "In a manner of speaking. The real Mardy Watt would never have asked me for a ruler at registration – you'd have just taken it."

"Is that so?"

"Of course! She was far too polite."

Mardy didn't know whether to hug Hal in gratitude or just punch him. Remembering what had happened with the red-haired boy earlier, however, she did neither. Besides, time was short. Hal might be able to see her now, but who knew how long that would last?

"Hal?"

"What is it?"

"Listen to me!" she said, almost shouting. She saw that Hal was already having to strain to hear her. "I don't have long. Has Rachel Fludd been in school today?"

"She's off sick. Mrs Yarrow said she might be gone for weeks. What do you want Rachel for? I thought you couldn't stand her."

Hal was looking at her with a mixture of incomprehension, fear and plain curiosity. Mardy could feel herself fading before his eyes, like a photo left too long in sunlight.

"I'll tell you, but— Hal, you won't stop believing in me, will you?"

"Of course I won't. I'm your best friend, aren't I?"

"Only I think – I hate to say this, Hal – but I *think* I'm going to need your help."

5 DOUBTFUL THOMAS

HAL WAS WIDE awake. He knew that because he had just pinched himself and it hurt. He sat on the bench under the larch tree, right in the middle of the playground, and blinked. Everything seemed normal enough. Twenty minutes to the bell. Information technology to come, then swimming (but Hal had athlete's foot and a doctor's note to prove it) and home. Fifty feet from where he sat he could see Mardy Watt quite plainly. She was chatting to Kylie Andrews and Kylie's little friend with the spots whose name he could never remember. Mardy wasn't saying much, but neither Kylie nor her friend seemed to find anything odd about her. The whole scene was perfectly – almost painfully – normal.

But if what he had just witnessed was real, then the creature calling itself Mardy was nothing of the kind, but an imposter, a double, a *Fetch*. And the real Mardy had been reduced to a pitiful ghost. Only two minutes ago she had been here, standing in front of the larch tree. Worse, he had seen the larch tree *through* her, every gnarl and knot. She had been pleading with him to help save her life.

Mardy had told Hal everything. Unless he helped her, she would fade away entirely, from this world to another called Uraniborg. No one would notice because the Fetch would still be there, carrying on her life. But soon the Fetch itself would sicken and die, and then Mardy's fate would be sealed. An eternity of slavery for Uraniborg's Mayor. And only Hal knew about it.

It was strange. It was a lot to take in.

Hal coughed and wiped his nose. There was no point in panicking, he told himself. He had to think this over carefully, as if it were a chess problem, and work out the best move. And the first question was this (the thought entered his head quite unbidden): could he be sure that person he had just been talking to *was* the real Mardy? It had looked and sounded like her, of course – but Mardy did not make a habit of floating around the playground like a demented soap bubble. The real Mardy Watt was about as ghostly as a sausage. Wasn't it more likely that the whole episode was some delusion of his own? A unusually lifelike daydream? Not a very pleasant thought that – but a much more plausible one, surely?

The thoughts came faster now, weaselling doubt into his mind. Why was he worrying about Mardy at all? Wasn't Mardy over there right now, in fact, talking to

Kylie? She was behaving a little oddly, but that could be explained a lot of other ways – more likely ways. Their row of the previous day had something to do with it, probably.

Soon, Hal had almost convinced himself that the whole thing had been some kind of dream. But still he wasn't happy and it was difficult to say why. The nearest he could get was by thinking of the way he sometimes got swept along in the lunch queue when his mind was elsewhere, so that he ended up with chicken when he had meant to have pizza. His thoughts were being carried along like that now. When Mardy had been standing in front of him, he had *known* it was her – the real Mardy. The creature that had sat next to him in class had no more of Mardy in it than a waxwork. He had been quite certain, then. But something – or someone – had got in behind his thoughts and begun to push them the other way. It was a creepy feeling.

Hal looked all around him. The children were playing – it was still fifteen minutes to the bell – and Mr Davies, the sports teacher on playground duty, was warming himself up with a few stretching exercises. The Fetch itself had left Kylie and was tying its shoelace on the steps to the hall. No one seemed to be aware of Hal or his thoughts. Glancing up at the school building he saw the head's office, just above the chemistry lab. There was Mr Shute, staring down at the playground with a severe and distant expression. His office glowed warmly, far above the chilly turmoil of the playground. Mr Shute was closer to God up there and perhaps a little bit of godliness rubbed off. Mr Bartok, the caretaker, was up a ladder again, fixing some kind of aerial to the roof of media studies. Mardy – or rather the Fetch – had finished tying its laces and was watching the operation, hands in pockets. It was standing very still and normally Hal would have said it looked thoughtful; but that did not seem the right word. Its stillness was not a living stillness. It was the stillness of a parked car.

"Find Rachel." That's what Mardy had told him. "Rachel's the only one who can help."

Those had been Mardy's last words before she had... faded out. Hal remembered the moment with a shudder. One moment Mardy had been telling him all about the War Memorial, about the Fetch and Uraniborg. She had been a changed Mardy, of course, thin and translucent, but *there*. The next moment he had seen a sudden look of horror come over her pale face and she had grabbed for his arm. He had felt her hand brush against him as lightly as a leaf. And suddenly he had been alone, with those final words echoing in his head. Find Rachel Fludd. But *where*? No one had any idea where she lived.

Hal went to the school office. He did not think he could face sitting next to the Fetch again. Even if the thought of it had not made him feel sick, he would not be able to disguise his knowledge of what it was. And it seemed important to keep that knowledge secret. Besides, the office was where the computers were.

Mrs Pugh, the secretary, was making some peppermint tea. Seeing Hal's face she gave him a cup with three sugars. Hal thanked her in a sickly way.

"I don't feel well," he confessed.

Mrs Pugh looked him up and down. Hal was not one of her regulars. If he said he was ill (and he certainly looked it), he was probably telling the truth.

"Let me see if I can track down the nurse," she said. She dialled a number on the internal phone, but got no reply. "Wait here, I'll just pop to the staffroom."

She left briskly, trailing peppermint-scented air. Hal waited ten seconds, in case she came back. Then he moved swiftly to the other side of Mrs Pugh's desk, where her computer was displaying the budget for this year's buildings maintenance. Hal did not hesitate. Within seconds he had located the files containing pupils' names and addresses. He typed in FLUDD, RACHEL and clicked. At that moment he heard footsteps outside. Hal froze, as a woman's silhouette showed through the frosted glass. For a moment everything was in a state of awful suspension. Then whoever it was changed her mind about entering, and the steps faded away towards the classrooms.

Hal breathed out slowly. A box had appeared on the screen:

FLUDD, RACHEL
69 TANGLEWOOD TERRACE
THE BUTTS

No telephone number was listed. Hal memorised the address, then hastily restored the screen to its original state. By the time Mrs Pugh and the school nurse entered he was sitting delicately on the edge of a chair, looking strangely flushed. His pulse was racing, too. The nurse, who was kind, made him finish his tea while she telephoned his parents. However, Mr and Mrs Young were out, as Hal had guessed and hoped.

"It's all right," he said heroically. "I only live up Bellevue Road. I can walk home."

"Are you sure?" said Mrs Pugh anxiously. "I don't think we should send you to an empty house when you're ill."

"My mum will be back from work in half an hour. It'll be fine, I promise."

So Hal escaped from school early. He was sure that no one saw him go. Not the Fetch (busy drawing Venn diagrams), nor Mr Shute (writing a report on truancy for the school governors), nor even Mr Bartok. Hal spotted Mr Bartok as he slipped through the school gates; the caretaker was carrying a rusty bicycle from the cycle rack and seemed oblivious of everything but the danger of getting oil on his overalls.

Hal stepped into the road and the gate clicked shut behind him. An electric lock slid into place. In school hours the gate could only be opened by using a button in the office, or by punching a secret code into a keypad. These were more of Mr Shute's security measures. But locks probably wouldn't be much use against the Mayor, Hal thought grimly.

He made his way down the road, past his own house. At the park he turned left, up a gravel alley behind some shops, and emerged three minutes later halfway down Mersea Hill. From there he had a view of the town's edge, a spire and the Industrial estate nudging in among the fields of Holstein cattle. Flat land ran to the horizon, where a sudden range of pointed hills ringed the view as neatly as a picket fence. The World's End hills, Hal had always called them. When he was younger he had refused to believe that anything beyond them could even exist.

He made his way down the hill towards The Butts. It was not a part of town he knew well. One hundred and fifty years earlier it had been pastureland, almost encircled by a long and lazy loop of river. Then an industrialist had opened a shoe factory nearby and (being an industrialist of the enlightened Victorian type) had built houses for his workers – small but sound and with good drains. The factory had long since shut down, but The Butts remained a place apart, cut off from the rest of the town. There never seemed any reason to go there – unless you were looking for someone.

Hal stopped at a newsagent's. He bought some gum, but not before sneaking a look at a local road map. Tanglewood Terrace was easy to find, near the centre of The Butts and right next to the Church of St Thomas, which must be the spire he had seen from the hill. Even from the shop he could spot the weathervane, black as a crow's foot. He took the road before him, which led directly towards it. The street was an unassuming one: terraces of ten or so houses each, with now and then a brick archway between, through which Hal saw here a washing line or rabbit hutch, there a skateboard, a caravan on bricks, a vegetable plot. After a hundred yards the road bulged out to make room for a roundabout and an off-licence, a pet grooming parlour, a dry cleaner and a general store. There was a bus stop too, and two more roads that branched off from the first. Hal looked again for the church spire – and had a surprise. The road he had walked down had been straight – dead straight – and when he had begun it had pointed him directly to the Church of St Thomas. Yet now the church had somehow drifted thirty degrees to the left.

It was strange – Hal did not usually make mistakes of that kind. He looked back. The road behind was as taut as a wire. At its far end he could see the traffic passing. There were distant people walking along it, too, though he had passed no one on his way.

Hal reasoned with himself. Which was more likely – that he should have made a simple navigation error, or that a bulky Victorian place of worship should have picked itself up, transepts and all, and wandered from one street to another?

There was only one answer, if you put it like that.

One of the new, branching roads now led to the church. Cautiously, and with a last look round to be sure of his bearings, Hal started along it. Very quickly the road came to seem familiar. It had the same neat terraces and the same grass verges as the first road. The Victorian industrialist who had built The Bulls might have been enlightened but he obviously lacked much sense of variety. Every house was an identical size, with windows and door painted in combinations of the same four colours: dark green, dark brown, dark purple or dark grey, each drearier than the last. The colour sequences seemed to be repeated randomly and Hal (who liked puzzles) wondered whether they could be made into a kind of code, like the DNA molecules he had read about in *Scientific American*. He began to keep a count of the passing colours and so did not notice as the church spire again began to veer slowly to the left...

Abruptly, he was at the street's end. Before him lay a strip of grassland with slides and swings, then the fenced river, which curled round on either side to make The Butts an almost-island. The Church of St Thomas, and Tanglewood Terrace beside it, now stood far to his left and as distant as ever. Hal began to feel seriously worried – and angry too. It was the same feeling he had had back in the playground, that his thoughts were being pushed – ever so gently, but with the firmness of an arm lock – away from places where *someone* did not want them to go. Why else would he have got so caught up in coding the colours of people's windows, when he was really on a life-or-death errand to find Rachel Fludd?

He clenched his fist, tried very hard to clench his brain too, and set off again – more warily, this time. He stayed with the riverside road, determined not to let the spire stray. He kept it doggedly in view as he walked the deserted pavement. Five minutes later the spire was definitely closer. Hal made a slight adjustment, taking a left-hand road a short way, then a right, down a long crescent moon of a street, lined like all the rest with the same neat and unremarkable terraces.

At intervals he found new groups of shops, huddling as if for company: more dry cleaners, more newsagents, more menders of radios and tumble driers. Each time he would wonder with slight surprise whether he had simply come round in a circle, so familiar did they appear. Then he would see some reassuring difference in the order of the shops or the names painted over the doors. The only things they all had in common was that they were small, shabby and shut. Friday must be half-day closing in The Butts, he thought – rather uneasily, for the solitude of the place was growing oppressive. The spire still lay ahead of him, though none of the roads ever seemed to lead to it quite directly, and Hal found that it almost always hung a little to the left. Nor, beyond a certain point, did it get any closer. That was the most frustrating thing of all. Just as he came close enough to the church to pick out the tiles of the roof, a new row of terraces would thrust itself between him and his destination, and he would be forced to slog its length, watching the spire recede into the grey clouds. It made him want to scream! If only there weren't always one more beckoning corner to turn...

And then – quite suddenly – he turned a corner and found himself back on the main road again. An articulated lorry rasped past with a shuddering wake of vile air. The noise made Hal realise just how eerily quiet The Butts had been, and how he too had been quieted by its multiple silences. The Butts, he saw, had turned him in one vast and complex circle. It had then spat him out like a pip. The spire had contrived to avoid him, and Tanglewood Terrace and Rachel's house had tucked themselves into the spire's shadow.

Hal turned on his heel.

"The witch girl refuse to see you, did she? I'm not surprised."

That voice – it was Mardy's! And there was Mardy herself, leaning against a No Parking sign not ten feet away. She was smiling at him in that provoking way of hers and for a moment it flashed through Hal's head that this whole adventure had been nothing but an elaborate practical joke at his expense. Then he looked into her eyes – as flat and treacherous as sheet ice – and knew that the person standing before him was not Mardy Watt nor any other human being. There was no point in pretending.

"You're the Fetch. Aren't you?"

The Fetch stepped forward and held out its hand, smiling unpleasantly. "Pleased to meet you, Hal."

Hal had to force himself not to turn and run. The creature was *too* much like Mardy. At the same time he was thinking furiously: What's it doing here? Did it follow me? He forced himself to touch its outstretched hand.

"It's cold," he said. "Your hands are cold like clay."

"If I hadn't been waiting here for the last half hour, you'd have found me warm enough," the Fetch retorted. "Don't *you* ever get cold?"

"All the same," said Hal stolidly, "you're not human." But even to himself it sounded as if he doubted it.

"I am a little world made cunningly, of elements and an angelic sprite," the Fetch recited in a sing-song voice. "Can you claim more? Or as much, my jumped-up ape?"

"You're blocking my way."

"You look lonely, little boy. You look like you've lost your way and don't know where to turn. You're out of your depth, Hal. Why not run now, run away? You'll be quite safe – no one will come after you."

Hal was strongly tempted. "What about Mardy?" he demanded.

The Fetch laughed. "Mardy is lost already. No point fretting about her – she's gone." It brightened at the thought. "*I'm* Mardy now," it added preeningly.

Hal was trying to remember what Mardy had told him about the Fetch. It wasn't alive, that was part of it – not truly alive. But what did that mean, exactly? If it could walk, and talk, and take pleasure in its own existence – what more was there to being alive than that? Then he remembered something.

"You may be Mardy for now," he said, "but really you're just a copy – and soon you'll start to wear out."

A flicker of doubt crossed the Fetch's face. But only for a moment. "Nonsense!" it chided him. "I'm immortal!"

"You weren't built to last, you know. Didn't the Mayor tell you that?"

From the Fetch's expression it was clear that he had not. It had not occurred to the Fetch that it might ever die. It did not know what to do with the idea. "You're wrong!" was all it could say. "That Artemisian witch has been telling you lies!"

"I haven't even seen Rachel. You know that."

"Then you're a liar yourself. I'm here to stay, Hal, so get used to it."

Hal stepped back. The Fetch was coming towards him, poking a fat, white finger into his chest with each step. Its face, calm as glass a minute before, was now distorted with anger and also a dawning fear. It looked less human than before, and Hal wondered how anyone could have mistaken this prodding automaton, this robot, this... *Fetch*, for his best friend Mardy. He was frightened, too. This creature might do anything, without pity or remorse – and who knew how much strength lay in those flabby hands? Hal guessed there was enough to tear his own head from his shoulders.

"You're a liar! Admit it!" ordered the Fetch.

Hal looked back over his shoulder and wondered whether to make a run for it. There was nowhere to go except The Butts, now growing misty in the afternoon light. Did he really want to be trapped in that labyrinth with the Fetch on his heels?

Then the Fetch flinched suddenly and gave a yelp of surprise. Before it had recovered, it flinched again, and held up its arm to shield itself from some invisible blow. It turned, still babbling threats, and retreated up the pavement at a run, up Mersea Hill and off into the lanes near the park.

Hal stood immobile, his gaze fixed on the place where the Fetch had disappeared. Now it was gone he was even more frightened than when it had been prodding his chest. It was only by a conscious effort that he stopped his teeth from chattering. But there was more than fear. Standing face to face with Mardy's double — at once so exactly like and unlike her — filled him with misery and pity for his lost friend. He missed Mardy Watt.

Darkness had begun to seep into the town. The cars cresting the hill had lit their headlamps. They streamed down, bypassing Hal and the road into The Butts, necklacing the World's End hills with ruby lights. The flat clouds were leaden, bruised, red. Hal, who had lived here all his life, was beginning to look at his town in quite a new way. He knew all about clouds and the difference between cumulus and cirrus and nimbus. He understood the seasons and the rotation of the planets, precession and solstice and equinox. He knew the first four rows of the Periodic Table off by heart. Nothing before today had given him cause to doubt that such knowledge was sufficient for most, if not all, of life's puzzles. But now he began to suspect that these solid facts were a kind of puppetry, designed to deceive and distract him. And that the other things – the ghosts, the old wives' tales, the bogeymen, the nightmares and their hatchling superstitions – were busy carrying on the real business of the world under his nose.

Something about the No Parking sign where the Fetch had been standing now caught his eye. A kind of stick, about the length of a ruler, was projecting from the metal pole, at the level of his heart. It had not been there before. Looking more closely he saw a twist of white feathers tied to one end by black twine. The other end of the stick had actually pierced the pole. Or rather, not the stick itself but something attached to it—

"Ouch!"

Hal pulled back the finger he had laid on the flint arrow-head – which is what it was – and sucked at the wicked heat-blister it had given him. Was this what the Fetch had flinched from? He saw now that this arrow was not the only one. Others lay scattered in the road beyond and several were sticking out from a nearby garden fence. How had he failed to see them?

He turned to look back down the long road into The Butts. The street lamps had come on in the last few minutes. They were sparsely placed, each lamp in its own island of amber light. A girl stood directly under one of the lamps, some fifty yards away. She was leaning casually on what Hal saw at once must be a bow and was shaking her head in obvious exasperation. It was Rachel Fludd.

"COME HERE, HAL!" Rachel called in a voice that was low but penetrating. She beckoned to him. "Get off the main road! It may come back!"

Hal did as he was told, pausing to take a last look at the arrow that had given him the blister. To his amazement, he saw water dripping from the feathers in its tail and heard the blunt crackle of thawing ice. It was not heat that had blistered his finger but searing cold. The arrow — all the arrows — were melting. Soon there would be no sign that they had ever existed.

"Hal! Are you coming or not?"

He moved up the road towards Rachel. She was dressed in a thick, hooded winter coat that fell almost to her ankles and her face peered out at him palely, like a full moon. The silver bow in her hand seemed bizarre and out of place, Hal thought, in such an unremarkable terraced street. But then he stopped and shivered, for he had glanced to right and left and seen, at every window, more faces — pale faces with shimmering dark hair. He saw only faces. Their bodies, if they had them, were lost in shadow. Each looked at him with the glassy, detached curiosity of a star, chronicling the world from its own chilly sphere. Hal was standing in his home town, thirty minutes' walk from his own front door, but seeing those faces he had never felt so unutterably lonely, nor been so aware of the measureless infinity of space above his head.

"So Mardy told you about me," said Rachel with a sigh. She saw Hal stare at the bow shimmering in her hand and shrugged. "We can do without this now." She let it fall to the road, where the silver shattered into a thousand splinters of ice. The golden string which had sent those flint arrows and put the Fetch to flight melted at once, leaving a rainbow smear of oil on the tarmac.

Hal was trying very hard not to show how frightened he was. He suspected that Rachel already despised him and if he was to succeed he needed her co-operation. "You know what happened to Mardy, don't you?"

Rachel nodded. "I saw you talking to her Fetch just now. The process is well advanced, I see."

"Then you'll know that she – Mardy – needs us. She came to see me earlier."

"To see *you*?" asked Rachel with undisguised surprise.

"Yes, but I could hardly see *her*, that was the point. She was fading out somehow, Rachel. You know what

I mean. She said you told her – about Uraniborg. And she said you were the only person who could help..."

Hal had not been as eloquent as he had intended. Rachel's gaze – ironic, quizzical, hostile even – was a hard thing to talk through and it did not falter. But there was no choice other than to go on.

"I don't understand a tenth of it – but you do. Whoever's done this to Mardy, he and you are the same kind."

"Ha!" said Rachel bitterly. "And just what kind is that, then?"

She was clearly ready to be offended by any reply Hal might offer, but reply he must. "You're the magical kind, Rachel Fludd. You can set protections on your home so that it can't be found. You can drive away the Fetch with weapons that melt away to nothing. You—"

"No need for a speech! I always thought you might have a bit of the preacher in you, and I was right." But she sounded quite pleased, Hal thought, as if he had passed some kind of test by speaking so plainly. She added: "Embarrassment's the first barrier, and you'd be surprised how many fall at it. Most people refuse to notice magic – they're terrified of looking foolish."

"That's never bothered me much."

"I can see that," said Rachel wryly. "And maybe Mardy isn't so stupid trusting you after all. But you're too late, Hal. I saw that Fetch and the signs are plain."

"The signs? What are they?"

"You'd better come to my house," said Rachel. "The Butts is fairly safe, but the Mayor still has some spies floating about in the upper air. Artemisia has been under siege for almost two hundred years, you know."

With this cryptic speech she took Hal further down the road towards the spire of St Thomas's and, finding a kink in the road Hal had not perceived before, led him to the door of the church itself. It was a grim building, buttressed with thick brick pillars, and the text on the noticeboard outside seemed (from the sidelong glance Hal gave it) to be forecasting a painful fate for wrongdoers of every description. But his attention was taken up with the four angels set into niches along the building's length. They were all beautiful, all severe. Each was carved from stone, but whichever one he looked at he had the impression that the other three were shifting slightly, turning for a better view or just moving their stony weight from foot to foot. Each carried a weapon: bow, spear, slingshot, leaded net. Rachel's comment about Artemisia being under siege came back to him and he thought he would never dare attack a place so garrisoned.

"Here's the place," said Rachel, stopping at the house next to the church. In fact the house seemed to be *part* of the church: it was faced with the same red sandstone blocks and the walls looked as if they were a foot thick. Rachel dug into her coat pocket and found a remarkably ordinary Yale key. Opening the door, she signalled for Hal to precede her.

"Come meet my folks," she added with a twisted smile.

Hal had noticed a sign with *The Vicarage* written on it nailed over the door. "You're religious?" he asked in an exploratory way.

"You could say that," responded Rachel matter-of-factly. "My mum's a priest. Go through to the back, I'll be right with you."

Hal walked up a wide hall which led into a square back parlour with a tiled hearth and three-bar fire. Beyond was what should have been a patch of garden, he supposed. But even by the decayed half-light it was alarming how completely the windows had been obscured by holly and privet, by feathery evergreen sprigs, all pressing blindly against the cracked glass. Only in one high corner was the early moon visible, moored in a current of drifting cloud. Had there been no other source of light Hal could not have seen the carpet at his feet; however, the standard lamp in the far corner gave out a niggardly orange glow. He waited for Rachel to join him and wondered where her family might be – for he had not sensed any other people house. When she failed to arrive, he peered back into the hall. It was empty, except for a cluster of ambiguous shadows from the high-backed chair next to the phone. He began to wonder if Rachel had abandoned him.

Then – although he did not see anyone enter – Hal was suddenly aware that someone else was present in the room. And it was strange: "Why aren't I scared?" he asked himself. But he wasn't scared – or, if he was, it was with a fluttering, breath-catching fear so close to pure excitement as to be pleasurable.

"Rachel? Is that you?"

"I hope that Rachel hasn't been too abrupt with you," said this new voice, and Hal saw that it belonged to a woman with a face as pale as Rachel's but far rounder. She wore round, rimless glasses and had a way of nibbling at the edges of her words as if reluctant to speak them. This made Hal think her nervous at first – an impression he would later revise. He noticed that she wore a clerical collar. "She can be abrupt, you know, and impetuous," continued the Reverend Fludd. "But try not to blame her. She's so very young."

"I'm young too," Hal found himself replying. He thought Rachel's mother might not have noticed.

"Of course you are, bless you," said Rachel's mother appreciatively. "And all this is a great burden for you, suddenly to be thrust into the midst of such a war as this between Uraniborg and Artemisia. Rachel at least has always understood the dangers."

"What do you mean – a war?" asked Hal. "I don't know anything about that. I came because of Mardy Watt."

"Of course you did," said the Reverend Fludd

98

again. "Please forgive me. We were all shocked to hear that Hannah Watt had lost another child, so soon after Alan. And that is really at the heart of this latest skirmish. We feel responsible, with their father being one of our own, as you might say."

Hal understood very little of this, but he had his terrier face on. He was not going to be deflected from the search for Mardy. "Can you tell me where Mardy is now? This double of hers is it some kind of clone? How can we get Mardy back?"

"Get her back?" repeated the Reverend Fludd in her nibbling way, as if his confidence surprised her. "Well, I don't know. So much depends on factors beyond our control. She'll have gone to ground, I dare say. Instinct will teach her that much. She'll be hiding out somewhere in the suburbs of Uraniborg. As long as the Fetch is alive the Mayor won't be able to summon her, not finally. But when the Fetch expires she'll have nothing left to anchor her to the physical world and that's when the Mayor will blow his trumpet. That's the end, of course."

"I don't understand what you're saying!" cried Hal. "All day long I've been hearing about Uraniborg and Fetches and Artemisia and a hundred other things I didn't even know existed. I always thought this was a quiet town," he complained.

"Quiet?" Rachel's mother looked at him coolly through her round-lensed glasses. Then she laughed out loud – a hooting scoff of a laugh. "As quiet as a hurricane's eye, that's what it is! As quiet as a pistol at your head!"

The light from the standard lamp seemed to be growing, if possible, still dimmer. Hal wished Rachel would come, for her mother had begun to be quite an alarming companion. He could no longer see into the corners of the room, and there were stirs of rustling movement there.

"Is there any way you can you help me?" he persisted. "Help Mardy, I mean?"

"I will not say it is absolutely hopeless," the Reverend Fludd opined, in a voice that implied the opposite.

"So there *is* something we can do?"

The Reverend Fludd smiled forbearingly. "Something to be attempted, perhaps. But let me explain the situation we find ourselves in and you will see the difficulty."

She beckoned him to her. Her finger was an ivory wand. "Some have called us witches," she confessed. "It is not the word I would use. But we shouldn't blame people for their ignorance when we've taken such care to keep ourselves secret. In fact, we are the Artemisians – the Children of the Moon. All over the world you will find us: separate people, a little out of step with humanity because we see more than you do and feel less."

"You work magic," said Hal bluntly.

"We have learned to prise open nature's secrets a little wider than you, yes. This small loop of river, which you call The Butts, is Artemisia – our stronghold. No one enters without our consent. As you discovered this afternoon, I think."

"I wandered round for half an hour," protested Hal. "No one stopped me."

"The perimeter of Artemisia will bend, but it does not easily break. You could have wandered all your life and still not found the Church of Thomas the Doubter. You are here because Rachel let you in, and that was only to save you from that creature of the Mayor's."

"The Mayor. He's the one who's got Mardy, isn't he? Is he some kind of magician?"

"He would like to be a god," said the Reverend Fludd shortly.

"Is he like you – an Artemisian?" Hal guessed.

"No! We Artemisians offend no one, ask nothing, give nothing. We are secure in ourselves. The Mayor will not be content with anything less than complete dominion. That is his disease. And there, such as it is, lies your hope."

She saw his incomprehension and sighed: "I shall have to explain from first principles." She drew a perfect circle in the air, her arm trailing a transitory light that set the room scuttling with geometric figures – triangles, ellipses and polyhedrons. "Number, proportion and harmony, Hal," she said. "Words out of your maths book. Perhaps they don't mean much to you, but they are the engine of the universe."

Hal looked at her blankly, wondering how she had managed to change the subject again. "What's this got to do with Mardy?"

"Have you ever seen an opera singer shatter a glass by singing a high note?"

"Only in cartoons," said Hal cautiously.

"The glass breaks because the singer has found its Reverberant Chord. Every object in the world has one. For a wine glass the Reverberant Chord may be as simple as a single note. For a human being, it will be something infinitely more complex. But find a person's Reverberant Chord and you will have mastery over them. You can enslave them or alter them to a shape of your choosing. You can copy them, as the Mayor has done in creating your friend's Fetch. Or you can break them like glass..."

"Are you saying that's what's happened to Mardy? That this Mayor character has found her... Reverberant Chord somehow?"

"She is enmeshed in the notes of that chord like a bird in a net," agreed the Reverend Fludd. "All her thoughts and memories, all her desires – everything that makes her who she is. It is her formula. With the chord, the Mayor can destroy your friend."

"Is that what he'll do?" cried Hal. "Destroy her?"

The Reverend Fludd shook her head. "Not quite.

He will change her. He will take her living will and shape it to his own. She will be an attendant spirit, a slave, like many others before her. Even now the streets of this town swarm with his spies. Haven't you seen them, Hal? Haven't you see the sky turn milk-white at evening with the flutter of their wings? Haven't you heard their whisperings at your shoulder?"

"No, no – that is... Where's Rachel got to?"

"Your eyes are only now beginning to open to that side of the world. We of Artemisia see them and we have laid protections on this place even the Mayor cannot break. Within Artemisia we have been safe. We are an ancient race and we have seen creatures like the Mayor come and go many times."

Hal looked around again for Rachel. Her mother had quickly ceased to be the vaguely reassuring woman she had first appeared. Perhaps the strangeness of the things she was saying had its effect, but those violet eyes had begun to glow like a cat's and the standard lamp behind her sometimes lit a frizz of loose hair to lend her face a startling orange penumbra. The room had grown darker again, too. The bars of the fire did nothing to dispel its stony chill.

"I said that the Artemisians are safe, and so we are – within Artemisia. But now and then there is a lapse. Martin Watt lapsed when he decided to abandon his birthright. He really believed he could survive without the protection of his own kind. Well, we are all paying the price of his folly now."

"I don't understand. Who *is* Martin Watt?"

"Your friend Mardy's father," said the Reverend Fludd impatiently. "He left Artemisia – oh, twenty years ago. For many years before that he had been our chief Recorder, noting all that passed in the world outside Artemisia so that we might turn it to our safety and best advantage. But too much contact with humans had a contaminating effect, it seems. The time came when merely observing events was not enough for him. He longed to live a human life, he said, with all a human's loves and frailties. Our persuasions made no difference. We could not keep him."

"So what happened?"

"Nothing, at first. Martin was not altogether unprepared, I will admit. He had studied the arts of deflection and he was careful not to draw attention to himself. He found a house, a wife, a job. They had children – a boy and a girl. I expect you couldn't have found a more normal-looking couple. Mrs Watt probably knew nothing about it, but for Martin that ordinariness was a barricade to defend himself from the eyes of the Mayor. He may even have deceived himself by the end. But he didn't deceive the Mayor – or not for long."

The Reverend Fludd fell silent. Hal was about to ask her to go on, when he was prevented by a loud and piercing laugh. And what a laugh! The throat that made it was as dry and cracked as a desert leaf. Close at hand, too – it came from the leather armchair beside the fire, where the cloaked shadows had conspired to print the image of a hook-nosed crone on the wall.

"Take no notice," said the Reverend Fludd hastily. "It's just the Olden growing impatient." She looked outside, her hair frizzier and more alarmingly orange than ever. The sky behind the sprawl of leaves was pricked with stars. "I must hurry with my story, though." She put her hand under Hal's chin – long, cool fingers they were – and lifted his gaze to hers. "Listen carefully. This is how it was. First – some four years ago now – Martin died. His car skidded out of control on the Mersea Road and he was killed. Whether the Mayor was involved I don't know, but it left him free to prey on Martin's children. We in Artemisia realised the danger right away. Their father had been an Artemisian. If the Mayor could capture them he might learn many things that would give him power against us, perhaps even here in our stronghold."

Hal nodded. "I see," he said shortly.

"We tried to bring them to live in safety here in Artemisia, but Martin's widow – a stubborn, ignorant woman – refused to let them go. Then, three months ago the Mayor seized his chance. No doubt he had been preparing his ground a good deal longer than that. To play anyone's Reverberant Chord, let alone that of an Artemisian, is a complex and dangerous matter: you always expose your own nature a little in doing so. But he did it. He grabbed Alan Watt out of his own skin as you might shell a pea, and in Alan's place he left a Fetch, a very sickly flower, which has been wilting ever since."

Hal stared. So that explained Mardy's brother and his mystery illness! He understood now.

"That's not Alan Watt lying in hospital," said the Reverend Fludd, reading his thoughts. "It's just a Fetch, a toy, a show. Yet the fact that it's still alive at all is a good sign. It shows that Alan, wherever he is, isn't yet fully in the Mayor's power. He must have found a way of staying out of reach, at least for now. No doubt that was why the Mayor turned his attention to Mardy."

"Mardy, yes! How can we save her? You still haven't told me!"

"There's only one way I know of. You must find the Mayor's own Reverberant Chord and use it against him."

"Then that's what I'll do! Just tell me how!" pleaded Hal.

The Reverend Fludd laughed. "You think we wouldn't have done it ourselves, if it were that simple? No, the Mayor will have worked out his own Chord. He'll be keeping that knowledge well hidden, count on it. Somewhere safe and secret."

"What sort of place?"

"An eggshell is the customary receptacle," reflected the Reverend Fludd, "but I doubt whether this particular enchanter will have paid that much respect to tradition. The formula for his Reverberant Chord might be anywhere – on a computer chip, on the back of a photograph, sewn into a shirt cuff. You must discover it for yourself, I'm afraid."

At that moment the clock on the mantelpiece stirred itself to action. There was a flurry of whirrs and creakings, and a little blacksmith took up his hammer and beat his anvil four times. Hal saw sparks fly up from the metal as he struck.

"Hadn't you better phone your mother and father?" said the Reverend Fludd suddenly. "They'll be wondering what's become of you."

Hal looked at Rachel's mother in surprise. For a moment she had sounded almost like a normal parent.

"But you don't have a phone," he objected.

"Of course we do. It doesn't take incoming calls, that's all. Just go through to the kitchen."

Hal did so, though he saw that the behind Reverend Fludd's concern for his parents' nerves lay a barely concealed desire to be rid of him. Perhaps she had told him everything she meant to tell. Before he was out of the room another of those mind-shredding cackles rang from the armchair in the corner and he looked back to see Rachel's mother bending over the silhouette of an ancient woman who was trying to rise to her feet, while the Reverend Fludd held down her shoulders with all her weight and strength.

The kitchen was not brightly lit, but it seemed so after the gloom of the living room. Rachel was standing in the corner, making herself an omelette. The feeling of normality was giddying and false.

"It's on the wall," said Rachel, shifting the eggy mix round the pan with a metal spatula.

Hal followed her nod and saw a cordless phone hanging by the hall door.

"How did you know I wanted the phone?"

"I'm surprised you even ask, after what you've seen," said Rachel. "The walls are thin round here."

"They look pretty solid to me," remarked Hal, remembering the four inches of dressed stone he had passed on his way into the house.

"I don't mean those walls. I mean the ones in here," said Rachel, tapping her head. "There's not much to call between the three of us – me and Mum and the Olden. Three sides of the same coin, you might say. Why don't you have a mobile, anyway?" she added, handing Hal the telephone receiver.

"My parents won't have them in the house. They say they fry your brains."

"The evidence is overwhelming." Rachel returned to her omelette, which was now beginning to smoke.

Hal phoned his parents and his mother answered almost at once. There was something about the way she said "Hello" – just a little too quickly, with just a little too much of a rise on the second syllable. "Hello? Who is it?"

"Just me. Sorry I'm late. I'm at a friend's."

"Hal! What friend? The school said you'd gone home ill. We've all been having visions of you dead in a ditch."

"I'm fine. I mean, I'm feeling a lot better. What do you mean, you've *all* been worried? Who's there?"

"Me and your dad. Oh, and Mardy came to check you were feeling better, the kind girl. But the truth is you've been bunking off, haven't you. It's not like you, Hal – what's going on?"

Hal was looking at the back of Rachel's head as she slipped her omelette on to the plate, next to an alp of mashed potato. Rachel was not giving much away, but he guessed she knew everything that was being said. He tried to catch her attention as she turned for the ketchup, flapping his hand and mouthing "MARDY'S THERE!"

Rachel raised her eyebrows. "Are you surprised?" she said and splodged ketchup over the mash. "Only it's not Mardy, is it?"

"Nothing's going on," Hal was reassuring his mother. "I just felt sick and I thought some fresh air would help. I'm at Rachel Fludd's."

"Who?"

"Rachel Fludd. She's – a girl I know at school."

"I see," said Mrs Young slowly. "Can I take it that your mysterious illness has disappeared now?"

"I feel much better thanks," said Hal stolidly. "I'll be home soon."

"Sooner than you think – your father's getting his coat now. Where exactly does this friend of yours live?"

"It's hard to describe," Hal floundered. "But don't worry, Rachel's mum's giving me a lift. I'll be home in thirty minutes."

"Make that fifteen. And I don't ever want to hear of you pulling this kind of stunt again. Understand, Hal?"

"Yes, Mum. I can promise you that."

Rachel was sitting at the table. She had poured herself some water and was drinking from a blue glass goblet.

"You'll be lucky, getting a lift off my mother. She'll be dealing with the Olden now. Besides, she hasn't got a car."

"Then I'll have to walk. But, Rachel, I've a feeling that if I leave this house I'll never be able to find it again."

Rachel took a long drink from the goblet. Hal thought she was deciding whether or not to lie to him – or just what lie to tell. "Expect not," she said in the end. "We have our own security to think of. We can't have people like you drifting in and out. Artemisia is not a charitable institution."

"I'm beginning to see that. I really am. In fact, I'm wondering why you ever came to our school at all. It wasn't to learn French."

"I thought my mother had told you. We guessed Mardy was in danger."

"You were watching her?"

"Like a hawk. Meant to be, anyway," she added regretfully. "Looks like I screwed up there."

Hal hesitated. "But wasn't that dangerous for you? I mean – what if the Mayor had tried for your Reverberant Chord too?"

"I wasn't without protection, Hal. In fact I was too cautious. I knew Mardy would react when she sensed our kinship and I was afraid she'd get some kind of schoolgirl crush' – Rachel did not hide her distaste at that notion – "so I tried to keep her at a distance, too successfully as it turns out. I'd assumed she would know something about Artemisia at least, but she turns out to have been as ignorant as a baby. By the time I realised, the Mayor had made his move. He's clever, you see. He'd obviously been watching her, too. And, of course, it's easier for him, Uraniborg Castle and your school having three dimensions in common."

"Meaning what?" asked Hal sharply.

"Oh, just that they're in the same physical place. Same place, different ontomorphic polarity."

"Come again?"

Rachel smiled apologetically. "I know. It's a terrible jargon. My mother, bless her, would be more poetic. She would say that the Mayor was haunting your school. But that might suggest he was a ghost, and the Mayor isn't dead, not a bit of it. The Mayor has an identity at your school as well, though perhaps you wouldn't guess it."

It took a moment for this to sink in. "You mean the Mayor might be someone I know?"

"Very likely."

"One of the teachers? Or a pupil, even?"

"I wish I could tell you, Hal. Don't think I wasn't looking! He knows how to cover his tracks, just like us. Only he's very curious, and that may be his weakness."

"Do you think I've got any hope, Rachel? Of getting Mardy back, I mean?"

Rachel looked at him sardonically. "There's always hope, Hal. All you have to do is find out who the Mayor is, discover his Reverberant Chord and play it – all before the Fetch dies. Oh, and do it all without the Mayor noticing. It's a chance all right. About one in a zillion."

"But you want me to try, all the same. I know you do. If you didn't want me to try, you and your mother wouldn't have told me all these things. I wouldn't even be here. You'd have left me to the Fetch, wouldn't you?"

Rachel looked at him in surprise, and for the first time with a kind of measured respect.

"Smart boy. And no doubt you think we're heartless for it."

Hal was not sure what he thought. "I think you use people," he replied. "If they're not like you – Artemisians – you only see them for what they're worth to you. You're using me now."

Rachel leaned forward across the table and said passionately: "We make the best of the chances Fate throws us, Hal. Just like your kind. *Using* you? Wait till you see what the Mayor is like: then you'll know what using means, child."

That word "child' brought Hal up short. As this conversation had been going on, he realised, Rachel had been speaking to him more and more as if she were an adult. This skinny girl, with an old-fashioned green ribbon in her hair, had been teaching him – and he had been meekly accepting it. He had somehow forgotten the difference between Rachel and the Reverend Fludd. In this house of shadows the difference was swamped by an overpowering sameness that settled over everything like soot.

"Remember what I said!" Rachel was pointing to her head, then squeezing finger and thumb together. "Paper thin, the walls between us three!"

He blinked, and looked again, and it was no longer Rachel sitting there. Her finger and thumb had grown longer and bonier, and their nails were tapering, dun-coloured claws. Her face was changed too. Her eyes, wheyish and teary now with age, had never been so spitefully mirthful, nor had her mouth been pressed so clear of colour. And the cackle, when it came, was like a ship's prow breaking pack ice.

"Moon people! Moon people! The moon has three faces, child – did you never learn that much?"

"Wh-where's Rachel?" Hal stammered. It was all he could say, though the look on the Olden's face told him the truth already.

"I am Rachel! And my daughter is Rachel and they are both me! If you had hung as I have hung, through the winnowing cold of space, and felt the years grow hoar-thick upon you, you would understand..."

Hal stood helpless with terror.

"If you had seen the slow revolution of the world, under stars that know no pity..."

There was something awful and mesmeric in the woman's voice and eyes. Hal felt the room grow cold about him as the unspeakable wind of space raddled his bones.

"We are the long-living ones," came the Olden's voice from far away. "The Longaevi. Our hearts are frozen hard and will not melt."

By now the room was quite dark. The only light was the little blue gas flame of the boiler on the wall, and that was hissing fiercely. Hal began to understand how distant the Artemisians must feel from the cares of human beings, who lived and died in a single hour of the universe's long-turning year.

"But we are not evil!"

It was the Reverend Fludd's voice. Stronger and warmer than the Olden's, into which it nevertheless seemed liable to dissolve.

"We're doing remarkably well, considering," added Rachel. "Good luck, Hal! Keep your wits about you. You've few enough to spare!"

"Be brave! Be wise as serpents! Trust no one!"

"Wrap up warm!"

At last, the wind was so fierce in Hal's face that he could neither see nor hear. There was something spiking the wind, too, a spiteful rain that stung his face and fingers. When the wind eased, he opened his eyes to find the darkness rearranged about him and less complete. The hissing blue gas flame was gone and in its place a line of orange lights ran from where he stood, into the distance. The black shape of a church spire cut the horizon. He was alone again, at the edge of The Butts, looking in.

The street lights were as ineffectual as ever, though he knew there were people on the pavement further down the road. Some of the same starry faces he had seen on his way into Artemisia had now ventured outside – a huddled constellation of them.

"They're seeing me off," he thought to himself.

"They've had their fill of me and now they want rid." Hal surprised himself by feeling hurt at his exclusion, though he knew that made no sense. Compared with the trouble Mardy was in, what did it matter how he was treated by the Artemisians? But he relieved his feelings by shouting aloud: "The feeling's mutual! Go twinkle at the bottom of a lake!"

The constellation of Artemisians did not reply, nor show by even the smallest movement that they had heard him.

THE NEXT DAY was Saturday. On Saturdays Hal's parents liked to lie in bed until ten or so, reading *The Guardian* and eating scotch pancakes. His little sister would find a cartoon channel and sit watching it till noon. Hal himself had a number of tasks. He watered the pot plants, changed the bedding for his pet rat and read three pages of the Encyclopaedia. Even this morning he did not swerve from his routine. He was grateful to put the problem of Uraniborg briefly aside. However, as he worked through the entries on Gainsborough and the Galapagos Islands that problem was already insistently pushing itself before him. The Mayor's Reverberant Chord was the key to getting Mardy back, clearly. But where could that Chord be found?

His first thought was to return to The Butts and ask Rachel's advice again. But he remembered his conversation of the previous afternoon and knew that would be useless. Artemisia's flexible border would never admit him a second time: Rachel had more or less said so. Well then. He had his own wit to fall back on and that was all.

"Mum? Dad?" he called ten minutes later.

"What is it?" said Mr Young blearily.

"Just me," said Hal, entering their bedroom with a tray. He had made them a fresh pot of coffee and stuck a sprig of leftover holly in the sugar.

"What's this? Peace offering?" yawned his father.

Hal smiled. "Sort of."

"I should think so," said his mother, adding as she took the cup: "You don't get off this lightly, though."

"I'm sorry about yesterday. Rachel kept me talking."

"She must be a wonderful conversationalist," said Mrs Young drily.

"She had a couple of things she needed to get off her chest."

"Did she now? And why have I never heard of this Rachel?"

"She's new. Newish. Doesn't have many friends. You've always encouraged me to make new friends, haven't you?"

"Within reason, Hal."

"Mardy doesn't like her," commented his father. "She didn't have a good word to say for your Rachel Fludd when she was round yesterday."

"No? Well, you know Mardy!" said Hal with forced jollity.

"She's not very free with her good opinion," agreed

Mr Young. "But I fancy there was more. You don't suppose she was *jealous*, do you, Hal?"

Hal made a face. He realised that this teasing was the price he had to pay for yesterday's truancy. With luck, by the end of it his parents would have joshed their way back into good humour with him.

"Was Mardy – OK?" he asked neutrally.

"She was quiet, as a matter of fact," said Mrs Young. "Didn't say much at all, then left without a goodbye. Not like our usual Mardy!"

"See? Jealous!" exclaimed her husband. "If you're playing one off against the other it's a dangerous game, son, take it from me."

"You'd have thought *she* was the one feeling sick," Mrs Young added. "Perhaps you should go and visit her, Hal."

"*Visit* her?" repeated Hal, appalled

"Yes, you know – that thing you do when you go to people's houses. What's the matter? Anyone would think I'd suggested open heart surgery."

"No, no – I think you're right," said Hal. "I should go this morning. Definitely."

Suddenly, it seemed not exactly the right course to take, but perhaps the only one. Apart from Rachel, the Fetch was the one being who knew what had happened to Mardy. Even if the Fetch was his enemy, perhaps he could trick some information from it. Besides, it had come to his house last night and he wanted to know why.

He set off for Mardy's without giving himself time to think better of the idea.

Hal had to ring the doorbell three times before Mrs Watt answered.

"You want to see Mardy," she said wearily, as if remarking that it had just begun to drizzle.

"Is she in?"

Mrs Watt stood aside. She looked inexpressibly tired – lined and grey. And behind the tiredness flickered the remains of a fear she hardly had the energy to feel. How much did she know, Hal wondered? Mrs Watt was not stupid. She must have guessed some of the truth at least. How much had she held back, pretending not to know or notice things, suspecting and being afraid to ask? Marriage to an Artemisian would be a slow torture, even if the Mayor didn't come into it.

The house had a disinfectant smell, as if Mrs Watt had been trying to eradicate some stubborn stain. Hal felt her eyes follow him up the stairs. His fingers were trembling as he gripped the rail and he hoped she wouldn't notice. Is she wondering why I've come? he thought. Why doesn't she say so? But beyond her first brief greeting Mrs Watt had said nothing at all. Hal wished she would. Something vacuous about the price of children's shoes would be enough. There was a charge in the house that needed earthing, and an everyday grumble might just be the thing to do it.

By the time he reached the landing Hal was almost

out of breath. There was Mardy's door. *Mary's Room* read the china nameplate, but Mardy had added the missing 'D' in black nail varnish. The door was ajar and it was dark inside.

"Mardy?" called Hal, remembering that Mrs Watt was still in earshot. "Are you there?"

"I have no name," came the Fetch's voice, leadenly. "You taught me that. I'm nobody. Now go away."

Hal forced himself not to turn on his heel and do just that. The transformation of Mardy's house made it even more frightening than Rachel's had been, because what had been transformed was so familiar, and the familiar things – Mardy's perfume, the nameplate, the stray copy of *Fave!* by the skirting board – still lingered there like cut flowers. But Mardy was gone. Her father and brother were gone before her and if they haunted this house now it was as unseen spirits. Hal felt a clutching at his heart. The feeling came so suddenly that he hardly recognised it as grief. He missed Mardy too much. Her jokes, her bossiness, her passion for Nut Krunch Bars. Even the things that annoyed him most he missed, because they were all part of Mardy, and Mardy was the best friend he had ever had.

He pushed the door open. The thin curtains silhouetted the top of Mardy's desk and chair, but the Fetch was not there. Hal could hear something turning restlessly in bed, a muffled folding of covers and sheets. He reached for the light.

"Are you deaf?" called the Fetch from under Mardy's duvet. "Turn that off and go away!"

"I won't," said Hal. He strode to the bed. It all felt bizarrely familiar: he was doing just what his parents did when they prised his sister out of bed on school mornings. He took the edge of the duvet and turned it back. The Fetch groaned.

"Don't look at me!"

But Hal had to look. The Fetch was ill – gravely so. Its cheeks had grown pale and overnight its face seemed to have turned thin and needle-chinned. The resemblance between Mardy and Rachel had never been so shockingly apparent as in this unhappy parody of them both. The Fetch had also grown weaker, perhaps. Or had its strength simply concentrated in those rope-thick shafts of muscle?

"You've come to mock me!" it accused him.

"No – to get Mardy back. You can help me."

The Fetch moaned and turned its face to the wall. "Mardy, Mardy! That's all anyone talks about! At least Mardy has a kind of life in Uraniborg. Can't you see I'm dying?"

It gave a sigh as lonely as the wind.

Pity was the last thing Hal expected to feel for the Fetch, but he felt it now. No one had asked it whether it wished to be created, after all. And now no one wished it to live. Hal wanted Mardy back, and the Mayor wanted Mardy entirely to himself, and either would mean the Fetch's extinction. The Fetch's borrowed flame of life would flicker out soon, one way or the other. If Hal could really have thought of it as a kind of machine, it would not have mattered. But the Fetch – whatever else it was – knew that it was alive. It *was* alive. Its body had just begun to learn the pleasures of touch, taste and smell: it was collecting its own store of experience as a bee collects nectar, dipping at every flower.

"It's your fault," complained the Fetch. "You're the one who told me. Ever since, I've felt the life draining away. I'm leaking life!" it added in sudden panic. It looked down at its own body, as if it expected to see its life dripping on to the floor like motor oil. Then, with a juddering, childish sob, it cried: "It's not *fair!*"

To his own amazement Hal found himself putting his arm round the Fetch's shoulder, and administering a soothing poultice of "There there"s and "It's all right"s. But all the time he was wondering: was it true? Had he made the Fetch ill, by convincing it of its own mortality? If so, he had not helped Mardy at all. He had only hastened the time when she would lose her one hope of return. If Mardy was watching him, he didn't like to think what she would have to say about it.

"I'm sorry," he said to the Fetch. "But it's the Mayor you should blame, not me. He may have created you, but he doesn't care much about your welfare, does he?

123

To him you're just a way of covering his tracks. You're only here to stop people noticing Mardy's gone."

"At least he gave me life," grunted the Fetch. "You just want to take it away again."

The Fetch's fury had shrunk now into hunch-shouldered sullenness. Hal knew the mood, as well as the tone of voice. They were both Mardy specialities.

"That's nonsense," he said decidedly. A firm reply was what usually worked best with Mardy on such occasions. "I haven't taken anything away from you. I just told you the truth. Do you think *anyone* likes the idea of dying? Do you think *I'm* looking forward to it?"

The Fetch stared at him, red-eyed. "That's different. It's not real for you, not yet. I've only got a few days left, probably, and you've got sixty years." It clutched at the sleeve of his coat. "Barring accidents..."

"You'd be stupid to hurt me," said Hal, backing away. "I'm the only friend you've got."

"You? A friend?" repeated the Fetch contemptuously. It was, however, unable to keep a certain wistfulness out of its voice. At any rate, the grip on Hal's coat relaxed.

"Get out," it said. "I don't want you here."

"But together we can do something to help you, I know we can—"

"*Get out!*" shrieked the Fetch, and with incredible agility it was out of bed and pushing him across the room. There was no resisting it, no more than a hurricane.

"Why did you come to my house last night, if you didn't want to see me?" spluttered Hal as he was forced back on to the landing.

"I didn't come to *see* you, I came to knock your brains out!"

"Great! Why don't you do it then?"

"It'll be a pleasure!" said the Fetch. It clenched its fist and lined it up with Hal's nose. But again it let the fist drop. "Because you're not worth the effort," it said, and a moment later Hal was alone on the landing, a door slamming in his face.

Mrs Watt was still at the bottom of the stairs as Hal came down them, his legs wobbling. She must have heard – something at least.

"Mardy's in a funny mood today," remarked Hal, hurrying to the door.

Mrs Watt nodded. "She's awfully worried about Alan."

Hal opened the door to leave, then stopped. Mrs Watt's gaze clung to him. There was a long, waiting moment when each seemed to be expecting the other to speak. Hal tried at last – but it was extraordinarily difficult to talk of magic to Mrs Watt.

"Only, she's mentioned some odd things recently. Reverberant Chords and, er, enchantments and such. You – you don't suppose she might be under a spell?" he stammered.

"Under a spell! What kind of question is that?" asked Mrs Watt aggressively.

"I only mean—"

"Under the weather, maybe. A spell! I've got enough on my plate without that kind of talk, Hal."

"I'm sorry. I didn't mean to offend you," Hal mumbled as he stepped outside.

Then Mrs Watt added unexpectedly: "You sound like that woman who came to see me just after Mardy's father died. She talked a lot about Chords and spells too."

Hal turned sharply. "Who was that?"

"Oh, she claimed to be a relative, but she was really some kind of religious fanatic. Dressed like a priest. She even had the gall to suggest taking the children away, into safekeeping as she called it. I told her to get off my doorstep or I'd call the police. 'They'll soon put *you* in safekeeping,' I said." Mrs Watt smiled grimly at the recollection. "She shifted then, sharp enough."

Hal would have asked more, but Mrs Watt had apparently decided it was time for him to leave too. The door shut firmly behind him.

Still dazed, he wandered back to the park. He sat on a bench and pulled his jacket close about him, and watched a toddler chase a flock of pigeons. The pigeons turned aside, then grudgingly flew off, clapping their rusty wings. The toddler began to cry.

Hal felt like joining in. There was no one to turn to now. The Fetch was his enemy. The Artemisians had cast him adrift in a world of magic he could not begin to navigate. And Mrs Watt? Whatever she knew she had chosen to understand in a way she could cope with – a way that did not involve magic. Hal did not blame her. Perhaps she had even been trying to help him with that doorstep reminiscence. But her defences against despair were thin and brittle, and he dared not push at them too hard. He stared in misery at the life going on around him, so invulnerably ordinary. From all this Mardy had been abducted, and only Hal both knew and cared.

Perhaps he should go back to The Butts after all, he wondered. Or the school: if that was where the Mayor was to be found. The Artemisians might not know who the Mayor was, but Hal was beginning to have his suspicions...

A whip-taut arm was suddenly locked about his throat. Someone was whispering in his ear.

"*What do you mean, we could be friends?*"

The Fetch's face appeared beside his own, lips drawn into a snarl. "Well, human boy?" it demanded. "What do you mean by it?"

Hal, unable to breathe, gestured to his throat. The Fetch loosened its grip a little and waited impatiently as Hal wheezed his way back to composure.

"Chalk and cheese we are, human boy! Apples and oranges!"

Hal managed to reply: "I only – *gasp* – mean we

both want something out of the Mayor. I want Mardy back, and you want a life to call your own. Only the Mayor can give us those things. He won't do it willingly, but if we can get a hold over him—"

"Fat chance!"

"—then maybe we could force him. It's not much of a chance, I know – but do you have any other?"

The Fetch thought about that. It thought long and hard.

"Why come to me?" it asked suspiciously. "Why don't you get your witch girl to help you?"

"I don't expect any more help from Rachel. She thinks it's a lost cause."

"Ha! She's got her head screwed on. What can we do against the Mayor? He's got this whole town under his thumb. All those cameras, the spies and whisperers – everything goes straight back to him. If he knew we were plotting against him—"

"He'd do what? What could he do to you that's worse than what he's doing already?"

"He'd think of something," predicted the Fetch ominously.

Hal thought that might well be true. But he couldn't afford to show doubt to the Fetch. "The point is this – we have to find the Mayor's Reverberant Chord. The Mayor wants to know and see everything, yes. But there's a price he has to pay. To live in this world he needs a body, a name, a set of memories – the things

128

that go to make up a Reverberant Chord. Rachel's mother told me he probably knows the Chord himself. He's found some way of keeping it safe, under lock and key. All we have to do is find the Chord and play it, and the Mayor will be history."

"All we have to do! *All?* To think I should spend my last hours listening to a lunatic! Let me ask you one question, Mr Miracle."

"Ask it," said Hal bullishly.

"Do you know what identity the Mayor has assumed? Here in our world?"

Hal's face dropped. "Well, no. Not exactly. I thought you might."

"Then you've fallen at the first fence, haven't you? Because I don't."

"Don't you remember anything of how he made you? Anything before you were Mardy?"

"I remember sitting at the desk in Mardy's room," said the Fetch, "writing an entry in your friend's tedious record of her tedious life. I remember bumping up against all her memories. Yuck – like finding a wardrobe full of sweaty clothes. And I remember... I remember the feel of the pen in my hand, and the wanting to know more, and the excitement, and – oh, all those other pleasures I'm going to have to put away because they aren't for the likes of me. But I never saw the Mayor, not in this world. I know *what* he is – not who."

The Fetch hesitated a moment, then added almost shyly: "I could guess, though."

"That's funny, because so could I."

"Do it, then. You first – I insist."

"Well," said Hal methodically, "it has to be someone at the school because that's where Uraniborg Castle is, according to Rachel. And we know the Mayor is a spy by nature. So who's been responsible for putting up all those cameras lately? Who spends most of his time looking out of his window to see who's coming and who's going?"

"Exactly!" said the Fetch, getting excited for the first time. "Just what I was going to say! If I'm right there's only one person it can be."

"Mr Shute!" exclaimed Hal.

"Mr Bartok!" exclaimed the Fetch.

AN HOUR LATER, as they walked to the school, they were still arguing about it.

"You're wrong," said Hal firmly. "Mr Shute's the one who wants to play God. Haven't you seen the way he stares out of his big headteacher's office all the time? That snooty 'master of all I survey' expression? Bartok's no threat to anyone. The poor man's a dogsbody."

"And you're an idiot," replied the Fetch. It was lagging as they walked and its breath was short – but it refused to be left behind. The thought of life seemed to have taken a new and firm hold in its mind. Besides, it needed to put Hal straight. "Can't you see that dogsbody act's a front? After what you've been through in the last twenty-four hours I'm surprised you're so easily taken in. Bartok is everywhere – hadn't you noticed? Mr Shute may sign the cheques for those TV cameras, but I bet they were Bartok's idea. He even has a house on the school grounds!"

"That's true," admitted Hal. Then he added prosaically: "But he would. He's the caretaker."

"He's taken care of Mardy all right," was the Fetch's sepulchral reply.

They had come to Hal's own street and the avenue of plane trees. The equal lines of chimneys, trees and telegraph poles stretched away like an exercise in perspective. At its far end the school slumbered. The air hung dully and above their heads they could hear the CCTV cameras clucking on their poles like roosting pigeons. Hal was trying hard to shake off the idea that the cameras were following their progress as they walked.

He found himself wondering again what had become of Mardy all this time. Was she aware of what he was planning? She might even be walking invisibly at his side at that moment, or shouting inaudible warnings in his ear. He squinted, trying to catch some wrinkling of the light around him that might indicate Mardy's presence. But there was nothing. The Fetch and he were alone on the grey street, with just the whirr of the cameras.

At the school gates they stopped. They had known the gates would be locked for the weekend, of course. They had even talked about it and had another argument. Mr Bartok's house had a front door on to the street and the Fetch had been all for picking the lock (it was sure it knew how) and sneaking in. Hal, with his mind still on Mr Shute, had remembered a place where a tree branch overhung the railing, and planned to climb into the grounds that way before making for the head's office. Each had been very scornful of the other's suggestion, but at last the Fetch had given way.

"After all," it had said, "if your plan goes wrong, nothing worse will come of it than a broken neck. If the Mayor catches me at his front door, there could be real trouble."

Which was about as gracious a way of admitting defeat as a Fetch could be expected to manage, Hal supposed. But at the gate they had a surprise.

"I don't like the look of *that*," said Hal. "Not one bit."

The gate was already open.

Hal tapped at the metal bars with his foot. The gate squeaked a bit and swung open further. "Will you come into my parlour?" he commented. "That's what this is meant to say. It's to frighten us off."

The Fetch snorted. "An open gate is meant to frighten us off? When we spent the last half hour arguing how to get through a locked one?"

"Well, yes. It's a mind game, isn't it?"

The Fetch looked unimpressed. "So you're going to turn tail and run now, are you?"

"Of course not! I only said it was *meant* to frighten us off. If we had any sense it would probably work."

"I can't afford sense," said the Fetch. "I haven't the time."

Hal heard the rasp in its voice. The Fetch was leaning against the stone gatepost, rather breathless.

Already it looked frailer than before. Whether it was fatigue from the walk, or fear, or the effect of being close to the Mayor, he did not know. All three, perhaps. The Fetch's time was running out. Even if the Mayor knew of their arrival there was no choice but to go on.

"Maybe the Mayor will listen to reason," Hal suggested doubtfully. "He can't be all bad, I suppose."

The Fetch gave a rueful laugh.

Once inside the gates, however, everything seemed so familiar, so *ordinary*, that Hal felt his guard relaxing. It became hard to believe that their lives were actually in danger. Could there really be an evil presence lurking in their grotty gymnasium? A warlock in the drama studio? Something nasty in the bike shed? Perhaps – but that wisp of thought seemed suddenly abstract and remote. All his senses told him that there was no real danger at all. Several of the teachers' cars were parked nearby, he noticed: they were probably having some kind of extra staff meeting. So the open gate wasn't much of a mystery either.

Passing outside the staffroom he even saw the meeting itself. He had an impression of Mr Shute, Mrs Mumm, Mrs Yarrow and about half a dozen other teachers engaged in earnest debate, while a screen displayed a list of bullet points that read 'Performance Target', 'Staff-pupil Ratio' and 'Benchmarking Standards'. He stopped and put his nose up against the glass. Mr Shute was holding forth on a subject both complex and unutterably dull, and several teachers were clearly having trouble staying awake. A little of that tedium must have passed through the glass to Hal, too, for he found himself suppressing a yawn.

"Come on," he said at last to the Fetch, who was standing impatiently beside him. "There's nothing here."

They moved round to the corner, out of sight.

"You feel it?" said the Fetch.

"Feel what?" Hal replied, taken by surprise. So relaxed had he become that he had drifted into a reverie.

"The nudging! Like a big soft hand kneading your mind, putting it into the shape it wants. It started the moment we walked through the gate."

"I was just thinking—"

"I *know* what you were thinking. You were thinking that there's nothing to see here after all. Maybe we got the place wrong, or the Mayor's really a fairy-tale, or we imagined the whole thing."

"It does seem very quiet," Hal admitted.

"And do you think *I'm* imaginary, human boy? Do you think this is make-believe?"

The Fetch grabbed his wrist and made him look it in the face. Even since the school gate there had been a change. Its skin, already sallow, was now discoloured with yellow and liverish blotches. It had also, Hal noticed, begun to smell. Not like someone who's forgotten to wash, but like a vegetable that's been left at the back of the fridge and started to rot. There was something so pitiable about it that he snapped out of his daydream at once.

"You see?" said the Fetch. "You understand?"

Hal nodded, ashamed. "It happened to me before, I think. Just after Mardy disappeared. I almost believed I'd been seeing things and that you were the real Mardy." He remembered the wandering spire of St Thomas the Doubter. "They use something like it in Artemisia, too."

"The Mayor and those Artemisians have more in common than either would like to admit," said the Fetch. "They're scrapings off the same plate, if you ask me."

Hal smiled, not only because he liked to hear the Fetch speak like that about the Mayor (and the Artemisians, for that matter), but because it had used such a Mardy phrase to do it! No one but Mardy talked about scrapings off the same plate. He wondered what kind of person the Fetch might have been if it hadn't found itself foisted into Mardy Watt's body and forced to wear Mardy's twelve-year stock of hand-me-down memories. Would it still have been so much like Mardy then? Or would it have taken its own place in the world and looked out at life with its own face?

With *her* own face, he corrected himself. It seemed wrong after that to think of the Fetch as *it*. Like doing the Mayor's job for him. And really, the Fetch had grown more human, even in a day. She no longer seemed like a machine to him. Perhaps being human was something you learned, he thought, like chess or knitting. Perhaps you got better with practice. He had not realised the true cruelty of Uraniborg until that moment. Not even what the Mayor was doing to Mardy seemed quite so wicked as this: the creation of a living, thinking being with no other purpose than to sicken and die for his convenience.

"Let's check out Bartok's house," he said, taking the Fetch by the arm.

"But what about your precious Mr Shute?" the Fetch protested.

Hal shook his head. "No go. The only way to his office is past the staffroom and the door's wide open. Anyway, you noticed the spell on this place, not me. So I bet you're right about Bartok too."

Mr Bartok's cottage formed part of the school boundary. The wall facing the street was trim and freshly painted in seaside colours, white and yellow and sky blue, with a display of souvenirs on the mantelpiece inside. The rear backed on to a small garden, hedged in and virtually barricaded by a greenhouse, potting shed, compost heap and three upturned wheelbarrows. There was also a little wicket gate, but this was kept shut with a twist of thick wire and from the way the wire was rusted had obviously not been opened for years. Hal and the Fetch peered through a palisade of beanpoles. There was a light on in the kitchen, but no sign of movement beyond the net curtains. The place felt empty.

"After you," said the Fetch. "This time I really do insist."

Hal straddled the wicket gate (he was just tall enough) and swished through the damp grass up to the back door. He was confronted with a sticker picturing an Alsatian, with the words "I LIVE HERE!" That wasn't reassuring at all. But Mr Bartok might have taken the dog for a walk, he told himself. Besides, the sticker was faded and old, and he didn't remember seeing Mr Bartok with a dog. Probably it was just a bluff.

"It won't put *me* off," he told himself, and tried the door handle. It turned and opened on to a dark, tunnel-like hall with rooms off it on either side. This was almost too easy to be true. It *was* too easy – just as the school gate had been. "Come into my parlour," Hal whispered to himself again. Even so, he waved the Fetch forward. The Fetch cleared the gate easily (she was taller than Hal) and joined him just inside the hall.

"Did you see the car park just now?" she asked excitedly.

"No, why?"

"It's empty," said the Fetch. "Told you."

"I don't understand," said Hal distractedly.

"That meeting you saw — it wasn't real. Just part of the brain-kneading spell. The Mayor *must* know we're here, if he's not bothering to keep it up any more."

"Then what are we wasting time for? Let's get searching for this Reverberant Chord while we still can!"

They moved forward into the house. In one of the rooms a clock struck the half hour. "Where do we start?" asked the Fetch.

"Anywhere a chord might be hidden! DVDs, CD-ROMs, floppy discs! Even books!"

Mr Bartok's living room was messy enough before they started searching it. Perhaps taking care of the school meant he had little energy left over for his own house. Perhaps he left things chaotic deliberately, to make searching harder. Either way, ransacking his things seemed to make very little difference to the appearance of the room. True, the Fetch managed to shatter a souvenir hourglass from St Malo — and Hal carelessly let a good-luck horseshoe fall into a forgotten plate of fried egg on toast. But these were small injuries compared with those Mr Bartok himself had inflicted on the room. And Hal and the Fetch had more excuse, for their time was short.

"I don't believe it!" said Hal after ten minutes. "Doesn't this man ever listen to music? Or read?"

"Perhaps he just watches television," said the Fetch. "He *is* a watcher, you know, in Uraniborg."

That set them off on a fruitless investigation of the television set, searching each inch for yellowing scraps of paper, hidden recesses, messages in marker pen, hieroglyphic scratches – anywhere a demon wizard might think to hide the formula for his Reverberant Chord. It was no use, though. Quarter of an hour had passed since they had entered the house and all they had done was break some ornaments.

"I'll try the kitchen," said the Fetch, picking her way into the corridor. Hal went to the window facing the street, the sill of which was home to yet more souvenirs. They made an odd assortment: a plastic flamenco dancer from Madrid (Hal shook her but nothing rattled), a Union Jack plate, a pit pony carved from South Welsh coal and snowstorm shaker with a model of the Eiffel Tower.

"Hal!"

It was the Fetch. Hal slipped the snowstorm into his pocket and followed her voice to the kitchen. The Fetch was standing in the doorway, but at Hal's approach she stepped aside. Hal saw a room that resembled the living room in messiness, though with a higher proportion of perishable goods. In the middle of the floor, slumped between a squeezi-mop and a packet of self-raising flour, lay a middle-aged man in brown overalls.

"Mr Bartok?" said Hal. There was a question in his voice, because Mr Bartok looked quite different from this angle. He had a bald spot on the top of his head Hal had never noticed before. But mostly Hal had never seen anyone look quite so deathly still. It was the stillness of a parked car.

"I don't think he's dead," said the Fetch. "Not exactly. More like – in suspended animation."

"Is it a heart attack?"

The Fetch shook her head. "Don't think so. This isn't natural. Someone's made him like this."

"*Someone?*" Hal began.

"You said it yourself, Hal. Come into my parlour, said the spider to the fly. And we walked in with our eyes wide open. I was wrong about old Mr Bartok, though."

Hal regarded the body at his feet. "No, I guess he's not the Mayor after all."

"*Mère!*" said a sharp voice at his back. "A long, elegant vowel, not a lazy diphthong. But your accent always was atrocious, Hal Young."

Hal turned. The voice was familiar, but even so he could not place it until he saw Mrs Mumm standing before him. She had on her sternest teacher's expression and was wearing a wide-brimmed hat. The mustard-yellow dress was familiar, but not the way it occasionally flowed and shimmered into something that in a better light (or a worse one) might have been a magician's cloak.

"Mrs Mumm?" gasped Hal, in surprise rather than fear. "What are you doing here?"

His first thought was that his French teacher had simply come to visit Mr Bartok and stumbled upon the scene by accident. Then her words and her shimmering appearance slowly started to make another, more sinister sense. "But – but *you* can't be the Mayor?"

"Why ever not?" replied Mrs Mumm haughtily. "And I've already told you, the word is *Mère*. You see? Mère, mother, Mrs Mumm – you can't say I didn't give you a sporting chance."

The way she said it made Hal blush with shame at his own stupidity, and even his poor accent. Something in Mrs Mumm's voice had that power, to make him feel the way she wanted him to feel, even when his brain told him quite differently.

"And now," she continued in her teacher's voice, "what are you doing in Mr Bartok's house?"

"We might ask you the same question," retorted the Fetch boldly.

"You might. I can tell you the same as I shall tell the police in due course. I was passing and heard voices and the sound of breaking ornaments. I came in to find two young ruffians standing over the body of poor Mr Bartok. So young and yet so homicidal! The scandal will damage the reputation of the school, of course, but at least I shall have done my civic duty."

"Body? Mr Bartok's not dead!" Hal cried.

"Isn't he? Then he's tougher than I gave him credit for. But we can soon fix that—"

Mrs Mumm raised her hand as if to throw something. Hal saw the shape of a spear, blue-grey and crackling with ice.

"No! You don't have to!"

Mrs Mumm held the spear in her hand. It was melting and freezing blue a hundred times a second, humming like a strip light.

"It's not Mr Bartok you came for, is it? You came to stop us. How is killing Mr Bartok going to help you?"

"You're right," said Mrs Mumm, considering the matter. "Too much attention is in nobody's interest. There are better ways than that to deal with you."

"You want our Reverberant Chords too, I suppose, just like Mardy."

"I already have copyright in this Fetch's," said Mrs Mumm dismissively. "Our clockwork friend is running down nicely, I see."

"I'm *not* clockwork!" coughed the Fetch.

"It really talks! How ingenious – and cries real tears, I don't doubt. No, I haven't time to calculate your Reverberant Chord, Hal. Frankly, I don't think your – shall we say, *limited* – soul would make a very distinguished addition to my collection. But there are other ways of restraining you."

143

All this time Mrs Mumm's dress-cum-cloak had been shimmering more and more. It was hard to stop your eye drifting in the direction of the shimmers, up towards Mrs Mumm's pale pretty face. And, once there, it was impossible to look away. Hal found his gaze locked. He could not see the Fetch properly, but he knew she was in the same predicament.

"It's rude to stare," said Mrs Mumm, with a thin-lipped smile. "I shall have to keep you both in detention. You will stay here until I decide what to do with you."

With a parting flourish the cloak reverted decisively to being a dress and Hal's gaze was promptly unfettered.

"*A très bientôt.*" Mrs Mumm turned on her heel and left, leaving Hal and the Fetch blinking.

"I thought we were done for there," said Hal after a few moments.

"Is she really gone?"

As if in answer, they saw Mrs Mumm walking down the road outside the kitchen window. She looked determined and rather serious, but about as unthreatening as it is possible for a teacher of French to be. Even now it was hard to believe that Mrs Mumm was really the sinister Mayor of Uraniborg, long vowel or not. Hal could even feel himself beginning to wonder whether the encounter of a moment ago had been a product of his imagination. "Mrs Mumm!" he wanted to cry out. "How can she be the Mayor? She can't be more than twenty-five years old!" But that was just the mind-kneading spell at work again. He was pleased with himself for spotting it so quickly.

"Let's go," he told the Fetch. "She's not going to scare us off."

The Fetch winced. "She doesn't need to."

Hal looked at her questioningly.

"Come over here and see for yourself."

Hal went. Or at least he tried to. But his legs would not budge. He looked down at his feet. They looked like feet, and the battered trainers they wore were certainly familiar, but he was not at all sure they were his. It was a most peculiar sensation. The feet were those of a stranger. "I think she's – somehow – given me someone else's feet!" he panicked, straining to move. "Come and help me!"

"I can't! My feet have been swapped too."

Hal looked at the Fetch's feet and saw at once that she was mistaken. She still wore Mardy's black shoes, just as she had ever since he had first seen her in Mrs Yarrow's classroom the previous day. "Yours haven't changed," he protested. "It's mine she's tampered with!"

The Fetch looked at him shrewdly. "There's nothing wrong with your feet at all," she said at length. "It's your brain that's unscrewed. Don't you get it? She's making us see it that way."

Hal opened his mouth to protest – then collapsed in despair. "Not again!" he groaned.

"We're in detention! She said it herself. No need for locks and keys when you can cut someone off from their own body. It's just like her, too," added the Fetch bitterly.

"So it's all in the mind?"

"Where else? Just think about it. What makes you so sure the things at the end of your legs aren't your own feet?"

"Well – if they were my feet, I'd be able to move them, wouldn't I?"

"And why can't you move them?"

Hal sighed. It was a paradox. "Because I'm sure they aren't mine," he said slowly.

"And that's what they call logic in Bellevue Road, is it?" scoffed the Fetch. "Come on, Hal, knowledge is power! Now we've seen through her there should be no problem."

"It's no good," said Hal. "I know you're right. I suppose they are my feet, really. But it makes no difference. I'm still stuck."

"If that's what it means to be human, I'd rather be clockwork any day," said the Fetch scornfully. And she strained and pulled and heaved at her own legs, until her pale face reddened with the effort. But in the end she dropped down, leaning against a kitchen cupboard. "No good," she admitted weakly.

"Congratulations. You are now officially a member of the human race."

The Fetch fingered a tin of luncheon meat.

They sat in silence. Mr Bartok's clock struck the three-quarter hour and did a little celebratory jig of tinkling chimes. A minute later Hal looked up.

"Did you hear something?"

"The clock. Why?"

"Not that. Somewhere up there." Hal looked towards the ceiling. "That roaring noise."

"A plane?" suggested the Fetch.

"No – not roaring, quite. More like a sheet being torn. Or water..."

"I hear it!" exclaimed the Fetch. "It's coming closer, isn't it?"

"Definitely – the whole house is vibrating now. Can't you feel?"

"I'm frightened, Hal! I wish we weren't on opposite sides of this filthy kitchen."

The Fetch's lower lip had a tremble worse than that of the walls. Even her limbs had begun to shake. Partly through fear, partly through sheer illness and desolation, it seemed she was on the point of breaking down. And that noise – like fabric ripping, or an engine grinding, yet somehow *purposeful* – was almost upon them. The thought came to Hal that Mr Bartok's house must have a Reverberant Chord and that the Mayor was now playing it. In a few seconds the room they sat in would be reduced to rubble.

"Hal!" screamed the Fetch. "Look at the sky!"

Hal looked, and it was all he could do not to scream too. For Mr Bartok's house had indeed gone. Not collapsed into rubble, but simply vanished. Above his head was nothing but sky – smoky, yellow sky for miles around, except for one circular patch directly overhead.

And there, the sky had a hole in it.

MARDY HAD BEEN on the run for several weeks. Or it might have been years, or maybe just hours after all. Uraniborg had plenty of clocks (she often came upon them hanging at street corners from handsome, wrought-iron brackets) but she never could find two that agreed, and she seemed to have left her own sense of time behind with her physical body. She had never realised how far time depends upon biology – upon the cycles of hunger, thirst and fatigue, the daily turning of light to dark and back again. Uraniborg had none of these things.

The geography of the place didn't help. Endless streets, all wearily familiar yet none quite the same, forked and twisted around her like a basket of snakes. Usually, she could see no more than twenty metres ahead before the next street corner. Tenements, warehouses, boarded shops she passed, sometimes a municipal park or a massy, granite statue. Now and then, aimlessly exploring, she came across one of the broad straight avenues that sliced the city, cutting into the twisty streets as cleanly as a blade. On these avenues the perspective was unimaginably long: lines of trees, lime, fig, even palm (she had seen all these and more) led in one direction to a vanishing point of smudged infinity. In the other direction the Mayor's castle lay, spired and turreted.

There was no sign of human life there or anywhere else. Only occasionally the awful silence of the city would be broken by a deep, gong-like bell. It was not particularly loud, but the silence into which it erupted was so complete that it carried easily – and it was so deep that, even if she had not been able to hear it, Mardy would have felt its echo fluttering her stomach. Whenever the bell sounded a great swarm lifted from the roof of the distant castle and swirled through the air in a mass before settling again. Birds, they might be, or insects. They were too far away for Mardy to be sure of anything, except that there were thousands of them.

Mardy soon realised that the castle was at the centre of all these avenues. They radiated from it like spokes in a wheel. At first, she had found them a relief from the claustrophobia of the twisty streets, but that relief soon gave way to other kinds of fear. It was along the avenues that the street cleaners occasionally rumbled, unmaking and renewing the city perpetually. She had been caught that way once with Rachel, but at least then she had had a body to return to. Mardy had no wish to discover what would become of her if she was caught now, an unprotected spirit. Besides, the view of the castle always made her want to hurry on, for that was where the Mayor watched and waited, and she was terrified of being seen.

When Mardy began her wanderings she thought that the city must go on for ever and that it must be entirely random in its plan. It was a long time (or it seemed a long time) until she came to a street she recognised – and that was because the clock on the street corner had a painted face she had admired the first time round: a picture of a frozen sea with wild swans flying over it. The mechanism of the clock must have failed entirely, for it still said ten to three and always would. After that, she observed and remembered more carefully. She began to gain a sense of the city's strange structure and to be able to navigate her way through it with increasing ease. Not only that, she noticed various points at which Uraniborg reminded her of her own town. The plane tree avenue where she had first seen Uraniborg with Rachel was one. It mirrored (or was mirrored by) the road where Hal lived so exactly that it made Mardy's heart ache with homesickness for her friend the first time she found it again. Not that it *looked* quite the same, though this street too was lined with stone-clad houses. Bellevue Road did not boast a water trough, for one thing, and Mardy could see one here quite clearly. But it *was* the same place, she knew it. And there were others: the dusty, five-way junction where she kicked up a parching waist-high mist as she passed; the half-timbered terraces that leant over the road from either side until their gables almost kissed.

Mardy began to think of these places as anchors, tethering Uraniborg and her own town together. No doubt it was through one of these that she had made her own entry to Uraniborg, shortly after her last conversation with Hal. But she was not sure: the memory of that time had grown hazy. At least she had managed to tell Hal what was happening to her, she comforted herself. At least there's somebody who knows what's become of me. Good old Hal.

But Hal can't do anything about it.

Uraniborg was flat, for the most part. Mardy sometimes thought there was a slight downward slope leading to the castle. But it was impossible to be certain. It was always easier to walk towards the castle than away from it, but that felt more like a magnetic pull – a dim restlessness that told her she would never be truly at ease until she gave up the struggle and laid herself, mind and soul, at the feet of the Mayor. How long would that time be delayed, she wondered? As long as her Fetch was alive on earth? Or not so long as that?

Then, one day (or one night, the two were indistinguishable) she found the canyon.

She almost fell into it. No one had thought to erect a fence or a warning notice, and the street she happened to be exploring (it was one of the twisty ones) was even darker and more shadowed by high tenements than usual. Suddenly it ended. The pavement, which had been leading her forward in a vague and purposeless way, simply stopped. Mardy peered forward, but the shadows spilled past her into undefined blackness, down to the centre of whatever earth Uraniborg was built upon. If Mardy had known more, she would have understood that this was the border of Artemisia, cloaked by strong and durable spells from observation within the Mayor's domain. As it was, it filled her with terror – the vastness of the abyss dazzled her spirit as daylight might dazzle a prisoner kept years underground. Yet that terror was mingled with hope. It proved that Uraniborg was not endless. There was a limit to it. And if there was a limit to the Mayor's city, there was a limit to the Mayor's power, also.

She retreated from the edge of the canyon, but not far. An appalled curiosity kept drawing her back to it. What would happen if she stepped off its edge? Was there an end to the canyon's blackness – a means of escape, even? Once, tentatively, she tried to dip her hand in. The air was thicker there – or rather the blackness was bounded by a strong but infinitely flexible skin, which pushed her fingertips gently back, as if she had touched a half-inflated balloon. Except that this was nothing like as tangible: when Mardy gripped, her fingers closed on air. The darkness only rippled a little, in an amused, contemptuous way. She thought again of falling into the void and this time saw herself dropping down into the darkness, numberless fathoms down, until the canyon's invisible skin caught and held her, helpless as a fly in aspic, conscious in the dark – for ever. Even slavery for the Mayor might be better than that.

Yet the canyon fascinated her – and from then on her wanderings round Uraniborg would take her there ever more often. Several streets led to it, she discovered. Mostly these were the twisty kind but they included one of the grand avenues from the castle, a sand-strewn avenue lined with date palms and spattered with camel-dung – though of course she saw no camels and the temperature did not exceed the dull tepidity universal in Uraniborg. Irksome little gusts and eddies ran along it, stinging Mardy's eyes whenever she ventured there. But at the canyon the wind faltered, and the dust it sprayed into the blackness was chewed and spat back lazily. Mardy would throw a handful in, just to watch. It was peculiar.

It was in that avenue that Mardy first saw the Mayor's slaves at close quarters. The first hint of their approach was not a sound, but a slight trepidation in the light – a flicker of shadow, here in a city without sun. She turned from the canyon and looked back down the lines of dusty palms, to the distant domes and towers of the Mayor's castle. A flock of small creatures had just lifted from the roof, stirred no doubt by the tolling of the city bell. Only this time they did not return. Perhaps Mardy had lingered too long within sight of the castle and been seen; perhaps her experiments with the canyon had drawn the Mayor's attention. Either way, the creatures were coming straight for her.

To begin with, Mardy was too terrified to move. The creatures were still some half a mile away, but they were flying at great speed and already she could see them more clearly. They were as thick and dark as a locust swarm, but they were not insects. They were the size of starlings, but she did not think they were birds either. Now she could hear the chirp and flitter of a million glistening wings, see the dragonfly iridescence of their tails, blue and green and yellow. And yet, and yet...

They were upon her. Instantly, she was in the middle of the swarm and the yellow light darkened with it. Thousands of shapes skimmed and frisked her, fanned her face. One – to her horror – settled on her arm. Instinctively, she brushed it away and as she did so she saw clearly for the first time what kind of creature it was. Padded, gecko feet; wings that folded back against a carapace of burnished copper; a tail turned over like a scorpion's to hang above its head. It was an amalgam of every slithering, sliming, fluttering, writhing thing she had ever shrunk from. But worst by far was the head. For the creature had a face – and the face had, all too clearly, once been human.

For an instant their eyes met. The creature's eyes were not dead, as the Fetch's had been, but the utter misery of them seemed to pull at Mardy's own soul and make it stumble under the weight of hopelessness and sorrow. Then the creature was gone and Mardy was fighting off countless others of its kind. The more she fought, the more there seemed to be – some insect-like, some flapping down on leathery wings, some pecking at her shins or sliding in coils about her feet. But all had human faces – and this was what sapped Mardy's courage most, for she knew too clearly now what her fate would be if she fell into the Mayor's hands. She would become just another mote in the darkening sky, another click and whirr of glassy wings in the castle roosts of Uraniborg.

They were herding her there. Mardy had not noticed at first, so busy had she been clawing the creatures from her and flailing at the air, but she now realised that she had already moved some distance from the canyon. The castle was perceptibly nearer: she even saw a glint from the conical tower of the Mayor's observatory. When the creatures swooped down upon her it was always to hustle her towards it. At that Mardy rebelled. It was panic and blind terror, but it was anger too that powered her through the clucking, chittering, burbling swarm. She tossed them down and tore at them savagely. They seemed to have no power to hurt her, but their weight and numbers pushed hard against her body as she waded, shoulder-deep, though a current of flesh and bone, towards the nearest opening off the avenue.

She made it at last. She ducked into one of the twisting lanes: the sight of the castle was cut off. And the creatures, stupefied with their own single-mindedness, seemed not to notice at first, but buzzed and fluttered uselessly in the broad avenue. Mardy took her chance and ran, at first past stalls and tents and buildings with ornate arches – all quite in keeping with the palm trees. Then the architecture subsided to the randomly grim style more typical of Uraniborg. A few dozen of the sharper-eyed creatures were already peeling off from the swarm and following her as she made the first corner.

She passed a haberdasher's shop (abandoned), a warehouse (boarded up) and a little courtyard of almshouses with a dry fountain in the middle. She recognised where she was. It was near one of the Tethered Places, where Uraniborg seemed to touch her own world. As usual, the resemblance was not a visual one, but something about this particular swirl of street, with its scatter of public buildings, reminded her insistently of the park. The air here was somehow greener, the light dappled with sounds that did not belong to Uraniborg but had filtered through enigmatically from another, desperately dear world.

The Mayor's slaves were gathering again. A score of them were circling Mardy, and several more had risen high above her head, where they were squawking out a signal for the rest to follow. There was nowhere for Mardy to go, no shelter of any kind, and she saw now that it was her fate to be hounded by these creatures until she either went mad or gave in and allowed them to drive her to the castle.

In desperation, Mardy tried the door of the nearest house, an imposing, four-storey building with black railings and steps up to the front door. As she had expected, the door was locked. The bell pull made a distant echo somewhere deep within, but Mardy knew that no one would answer. All these buildings were sham – no more than stage scenery for the Mayor's fantasies. In Uraniborg she was quite alone. She and the creatures now bombarding her were the only living things in this sprawling city. Except for the Mayor himself, of course.

She swung herself down to the pavement and ran. Of course, she could not outrun the creatures, but to walk calmly through their tumult was unthinkable. She came to a new street, back down a narrow, high-walled alley, then to a sooty tavern, into a junkyard and out through a hole in the fence, emerging breathlessly, almost back where she had started, in a kind of market place. The sense of the park came strongly upon her again, as she saw what stood at its centre: a white, pillared building like a miniature Roman temple. Only it was not quite *neat* enough. When she got closer she saw a filigree of abstract flower carvings on all the close-set pillars. Faces, too, on the square panels beyond the pillars. She squeezed through to look.

Immediately, the battering of the creatures ceased. Perhaps they could not work out how to fly between the narrow temple pillars. It would not take them long to realise that they could crawl through, Mardy supposed, but for a few moments she was free of them. She turned to look again at the panels on the temple. She saw people's faces: old, young, male, female, bearded, clean-shaven. *They* were familiar, too. And the one she was looking at right now was too familiar for words. It was a young man, thin-faced but with an elegant, unforced strength in his expression, particularly in his eyes. The eyes were looking straight at her. One of them winked.

A stone-white hand shot out from the temple wall. Mardy felt her own wrist being seized and at once she was yanked forward. She flinched and shut her eyes as she saw the wall of the temple slamming into her face. But the expected impact never came. There was a *glooping* feeling inside her brain, and then she was falling forwards on to her knees, opening her eyes, gasping. She was blinking in the light of a dim, moon-shaped lantern, into a face as well-known to her as her own.

"Alan?" she asked, astonished. She tried to say more but found that her tongue would not move.

"Hello, Spud," he said.

"DON'T CALL ME that!" shouted Mardy. "I've told you! You—"

He took her in his arms as she broke down at last. She wept freely, fiercely – not wanting to emerge from the luxury of it. Alan was well and he had saved her life. Wherever they were, it was a place to which the Mayor's slaves could not follow her. What need was there for more than that?

Alan, meanwhile, was smiling as he hugged her. But there was distress in his eyes. "Oh, Spud – Mardy, I mean – It's so good to see you. But not to see you *here*. Did the Mayor get you too, then?"

Mardy nodded, head still in his chest. "I *hate* the Mayor!"

"Of course you do. And now you're here perhaps we can do something about it. You're safe for now, anyway. The spell I put over the entrance seems to be holding."

Mardy lifted her head and stared at him. "The spell *you* put?"

"We'll talk about that later," said Alan hastily. "Now stop crying on my toga, Mardy, you'll give me rheumatics. Let's have a look at you."

Mardy stepped back and they regarded each other. A silence fell on them, almost as if they were strangers. Alan seemed to have become a ghost. He was as white as the temple marble, both skin and clothes. And the clothes matched those of the statues among which they stood. He was indeed wearing a toga.

Mardy looked down at herself. It was only now, under the gaze of another human being, that she had stopped to wonder what she looked like. Alone in the streets of Uraniborg, it had not seemed to matter. And it was a shock. Her skin was the same smoky yellow as the Uraniborg sky. Her clothes too – her rags, rather – were jaundiced and muddy-looking. If she had seen herself framed in a picture, she would have taken herself for an unusually podgy street waif, painted by a sentimental Victorian. *Come Buy my Matches*, the painting would be called.

"I know," laughed Alan, seeing her dismay. "You take on the style and colour of your surroundings. It seems to be a rule of this place. Perhaps it's because we're only half here and the city has to make up the rest somehow. But it makes good camouflage, don't you think?"

Mardy did not find it particularly funny. It was

somehow typical that she had ended up as a beggar while Alan was halfway between captain of the first eleven and the emperor's favourite nephew. Of course it didn't matter, not when she thought of the situation they were in. But it still wasn't *fair*.

She sat down on the floor of the temple.

"So what do we do now?" she asked flatly. "What have *you* been doing all this time? Back home, you – your body's in a coma. You've not moved for three months."

"I know. There's a part of me – have you noticed it too? – that seems to know what my Fetch is up to. The poor thing's being fed through a tube, somewhere. But three months! I hadn't realised it was so long."

"So you know about Fetches too, do you?" said Mardy in surprise.

"A little," said Alan, somewhat flustered. "Doesn't everyone?"

"No! Who told you? What else do you know?"

"Calm down, Mardy! It's not a competition."

"I didn't say it was! But – oh, I'd forgotten just how smug you could be, Alan Watt. Look at you standing there, waiting for me to catch up."

"I promise you I'm not," Alan protested. "I just happen to know a thing or two about Fetches and Uraniborg and the like."

"That's something you cover in A-level sociology, is it?"

Alan laughed a dinner-party laugh. "Not exactly. The truth is, Dad let me in on some of it before he died." He lowered his voice. "I think perhaps he guessed the Mayor was on to him."

Mardy was so angry she could feel her toes curling into the marble floor. "*Dad* told you about the Mayor?"

"A little, Mardy, a little. The least he could get away with, I'm sure."

Alan spread his arms innocently. As he did so Mardy caught sight of the mark on the inside of his arm. It was a little crescent-shaped scar from an accident with a soldering iron – oh, seven years ago. Only now it came to her with sudden certainty what that scar really was. It was the mark of his initiation. Alan was an Artemisian witch.

"You've known about the Mayor all these years! Why didn't anyone tell *me*?"

Alan grimaced. "You were very young. I suppose we didn't want to frighten you with things you weren't old enough to understand."

"Well, I understand it now all right! I understand that we're stuck here in a marble box for the rest of eternity. So thanks for sparing my feelings."

"Things do look bad," admitted Alan. "Uraniborg's no holiday camp. But I have hopes, Mardy. I've been working on a plan."

Mardy didn't want to reply. But she had to. "What plan?" she muttered.

"Not a plan, exactly. More of a strategy...'

"*Alan!*"

"All right – I'll tell you what I've been up to. I've been exploring and I've found a few things out. First, Uraniborg isn't all of a piece. Most of it seems to be impregnable, but in parts there are powerful harmonics that resonate with our own world."

Mardy was already confused, but she had an idea he must be talking about the Tethered Places. She nodded sagely.

"Elsewhere again the city is badly imagined. You can see it in the inconsistencies – like here, where there's a classical temple planted in the middle of the Dickens quarter. It doesn't fit, does it? When I see something like that, I know the Mayor's attention has wandered – and with luck I'll be able to pierce the fabric of the city and build myself a bolt-hole without his noticing. Like this one."

"I see," said Mardy slowly.

"Yes, most of the magic Dad taught me won't work here, but where there's an obvious weakness I can work with it and set up some Deflective Spells. I've got a couple of dozen scattered around the city."

"Alan, how much magic *did* Dad teach you?"

"Hardly any at all," Alan reassured her. "Just – you know – the basics."

"The basics. I see."

"That's right," nodded Alan. "But of course he did tell

me about Reverberant Chords. You've heard of those, I suppose?" he added in a way Mardy could not but find infuriating, though he evidently meant well. (Alan *always* meant well, Mardy reflected bitterly.)

"Of course I've heard of Reverberant Chords," she was able to say. "They're what the Mayor plays to make copies of us – to bring us to Uraniborg. They're unique – like a fingerprint."

"That's right," said Alan encouragingly. "But did you ever wonder about the Mayor's own Reverberant Chord?"

Mardy wanted to reply that she had given the matter careful consideration. But she had to answer with a muted "No."

"He has one, of course. Potentially, that makes him as vulnerable as you or me. The only trouble is, he's worked it out himself. And he's taken that knowledge and hidden it. That's allowed, you know. As long as it stays hidden, he's safe. But it's not hidden from me."

Alan waited for her to react.

"You're telling me you've found the Mayor's Reverberant Chord?" said Mardy ploddingly.

"You might be a bit more impressed," complained Alan. "People have been after it for years and years. But they've all made the same mistake. They've been looking for it in small, tucked-away places: books, tapes, microfilm. But the Mayor hid it somewhere big

– so big it was almost invisible. That's where he was clever."

"But not as clever as you, obviously."

Alan tried to look modest. "The discovery was almost an accident. I told you I'd been exploring Uraniborg. In fact, I did more than that – I made a map of the place. There's plenty of paper littering the city, you've probably noticed. I happened to be writing down a phone number when the Mayor played my Reverberant Chord, and when I got here I found I'd brought this along." He produced (Mardy was not sure from where, unless from the folds of his toga) a shiny, metal fountain pen. Mardy recognised it from Alan's last birthday. No magic wand could have impressed her more than this fragment of contraband reality. It made her sick with the desire of her own home.

"Is that the map?" she asked, spying a large sheet of dusty paper on the floor nearby.

"Have a look," said Alan. "I wanted to show you, anyway. You see, when I started to sketch Uraniborg I soon noticed a pattern. Look, Mardy – see *here*. And *here*." He stabbed his finger at the paper, but all Mardy could see were a lot of random lines, along with ten or so straight ones which might have been the castle avenues. "And look where the castle is!" He stabbed again.

"In the middle of the city," said Mardy, thoroughly confused. "Well, almost."

"Almost. Exactly. I knew you'd see it. Everything here *pretends* to be symmetrical, but it's not! Proportions, Mardy! It's all to do with the ratio of north to south, east to west, the way the streets curve round but never at quite the same angle..." Alan gagged through trying to tell her everything at once. "It can all be reduced to a musical notation, you see. Intervals, periods, pitch, amplitude. It took me quite a time to work out the detailed correspondences, but that was the moment of revelation – when I understood that Uraniborg *was* the Mayor."

Mardy wondered seriously whether living alone in Uraniborg hadn't driven Alan slightly mad. His eyes were shining and his words made no connection with her mind. Then she remembered that Alan had always talked that way. Also, some of the things he said did make sense – a sort of sense. Her beggar girl costume, she noticed, was changing, much as Alan had said it would. The hanging rags now looked considerably more like swags of folded cloth, and they were no longer the same sulphurous yellow but a rather interesting sepia. In these classical surroundings she might soon be adorned quite as elegantly as her brother.

"But how can the Mayor *be* a city?" she asked him.

"That's a loose way of putting it," corrected Alan, forgetting that the phrase had been his own. "But the formula for the Mayor's Reverberant Chord is written all around us – in the street plan and the architecture of Uraniborg. The city is made in his image. I've copied it down right here."

He unfolded a second, smaller sheet of paper, on which he had drawn a pair of musical staves. Both were black with an ants' nest of crotchets and quavers, swooping glissandos and sonorous semi-breves. The page resembled an orchard, in which each note climbed to a ludicrous height and was spread with innumerable branches, all of them heavy with dangling fruit. Notes higher than the highest squeak of a piccolo, notes lower than a tuba's grossest fart. They swam before Mardy's eyes.

"I'll accept your congratulations, if you feel like offering them," Alan prompted at last.

"It's very clever," said Mardy.

"Is that all you can say? Mardy, I'm not sure you realise how much work – yes, and dangerous work, too – went into this. I'm holding the Mayor's death warrant."

"So all you need to do," said Mardy, feeling her way forward, "is to play this chord—"

"And the Mayor will be at my mercy, yes. Our mercy, I mean."

Alan smiled slickly. Mardy, knowing her brother, wondered what he was trying to hide.

"So why haven't you? Why don't you?"

"I'm sorry?"

"Why haven't you played this chord? If it's so simple. Why didn't you play it ages ago?"

"I'd have thought that was obvious," Alan protested. "I've nothing to play it *with*."

"Oh," said Mardy. For a moment she had almost allowed herself to believe that Alan was about to lead her to freedom. Of course it couldn't be that simple.

"But there are instruments!" She remembered suddenly. "I saw them in one of the streets, not far from here. A whole row of shops selling easels and paints, and masks, and musical instruments too! There's no one there – we could just break in and help ourselves."

Alan shook his head. "No good. This chord is vast – you can see that for yourself. It has notes way beyond the range of any conventional instrument. Anyway, to play them all at once you'd need more fingers than a dog has fleas. No, the only way I can see is to program a computer – hooked up to speakers or something. I admit I haven't quite worked out that stage of the plan," he added mumblingly.

If only Hal were here, Mardy thought helplessly! Alan was all right for flashes of inspiration, but when it came to putting ideas into practice he preferred to leave it to others. She looked at him now, sucking the top of his pen as if he were doing a crossword puzzle over morning toast. While a part of her thought Alan's calmness of mind admirable, a much larger part wanted to kick him smartly in the shin.

"Alan – what's that in your mouth?"

"What? Oh, sorry." Alan took his pen out of his

mouth and wiped the end apologetically with a spare bit of toga. It was a habit he had been trying to kick since primary school.

"I don't care about that," said Mardy. "It's the *pen*. Look at it!"

Alan looked. He shook a drop of ink on to the marble floor, where it spread in a spidery way along the filigree cracks in the stone. "I don't see what you're getting at," he began.

"What's it *made* of?"

"Silver, I think. Silver plate, anyhow – I don't suppose Mum could afford to go the whole hog."

"Silver plate will do," said Mardy. "It'll have to do! Here, give it to me."

Alan hesitated, but only (to his credit) for a moment. He handed the pen over and watched as Mardy wrote on a scrap of nearby paper. Then he sat pained but quiescent as she unscrewed the top and disembowelled it. Out came an assortment of levers and springs, and the long, inky gut. Mardy pored over it like a priestess sniffing entrails.

"The paper with the music," she said, without looking up. "Give."

Alan gave his intricate chord a regretful look, but placed it obediently in Mardy's outstretched hand. To his horror she began to roll it up.

"Careful, Mardy!"

"Yes?" said Mardy briskly.

"I— nothing. It's just – I only have one copy of that thing, you know."

"Let's hope I'm right, then," said Mardy none too reassuringly, wrapping her own note tightly around the rolled paper. The scroll was hardly thicker than a tooth pick. Alan agonised at a distance as Mardy slipped it into the casing of the pen.

"Silver," she said, "is the one thing that can move freely between Uraniborg and our world. Rachel Fludd told me. That's probably why you were able to bring it here in the first place."

"Who on earth is Rachel Fludd?"

"A girl in my class – oh, never mind." Mardy screwed the pen top back firmly. "Now, how do we get out of this temple?"

Alan smiled that nervous half-smile again. "Where do you want to go?"

Mardy told her brother about the drinking trough near Uraniborg Castle and the way Rachel had used it. Alan knew the place, it appeared. He had come across it soon after his arrival in the city. But he was not enthusiastic about returning.

"It's right under the Mayor's nose!" he exclaimed. "We wouldn't last a minute."

"And your way we'll last how long? A week? A month? This story only has one ending, Alan."

Alan hesitated – and gave a long, resigned sigh. "A thousand endings, all the same. You're right, we ought to try it. Only trouble is, they're waiting for us." Alan jerked his thumb back over his shoulder to the wall behind him. He took a fold of the cloth hanging from his shoulder and rubbed at the white marble. To Mardy's surprise the marble rubbed off as if it had been condensation on a mirror. At once they were able to see what lay outside.

Or rather, they weren't. The temple's outer wall was clogged with the bodies of the Mayor's slaves. Wings, mouths, curling, snaky tails, bodies that tapped icily or slimed like snails' feet. There was no chink of light. And Mardy knew that behind those bodies were others, a heaving slab of them many ranks thick, all intent only on reaching her and Alan. Even more strongly than fear, she felt a powerful disgust, a sickness that began by being directed at the creatures outside but soon turned on herself. The Mayor's slaves could not break the magic of the temple wall, but their thoughts found their way insidiously into her mind. "Give up now!" they whispered. "There is no way out for you. You are the Mayor's now, you are one of us!"

Mardy glanced at Alan, but he seemed to feel nothing. The assault was directed at her mind alone.

She opened her mouth to say something undaunted, but heard herself intone dully: "That's it, then. We're trapped for ever."

"For the moment," Alan corrected her. "Your plan will have to wait, that's all."

"Some plan!" said Mardy, crumpling to the floor.

"No, it's a good plan," Alan encouraged her. "I'm sure I'll be able to direct the pen to your friend Hal once we get to the drinking trough. It's a risk we'll have to take, going so near the castle. I've been far too cautious," he added by way of self-reproach. "I think I needed you here to bring out my valorous streak."

"It might have been a good plan once, but it's too late," Mardy gloomed on. "Those harpies will never let us leave."

Alan thought about that. "I'm not so sure," he said. "I've been watching their habits, and they're none too bright. They never stay away from the Castle for long, either. I think they're too closely tied to the Mayor for that. If we wait long enough, there's a good chance they'll drift off. Hey, what's wrong, little sister?"

Alan had only just noticed that Mardy was now a soggy heap of despair on the tiles at his feet. He squatted beside her. "Mardy, what's the matter? We're going to get home. You do believe that, don't you?"

"It's so easy to say, isn't it?" returned Mardy with a bitterness that surprised them both. "If you're Alan Watt, it's easy to believe too, I'm sure. Everything's easy if you're Alan Watt."

"Now hang on, Mardy—"

"You've always been a luck magnet, haven't you? You've been lucky so long you think that's the way life is, one long helter-skelter ride. Did you never notice that it isn't that way for everyone? Me, for instance?"

Mardy blinked up at her brother. She could feel herself shrinking back inside her own skin, wrinkled and bitter. Her eyes, black with tears, would not cry. And all the time the creatures beyond the wall were dragging her mind for any source of doubt or resentment. Every petty distinction her parents had made between her and Alan came back to her, magnified tenfold. How his birthday presents had always been more expensive, how Mum would rally to any school play where he had a bit part and raise the rafters, while her own efforts on solo bassoon went unappreciated. How Dad had told Alan but not her about Artemisia. And how – how her mother had looked at her, that first time in the hospital. Her strange, half-resentful expression had puzzled her at the time, but now she thought she understood it. "It should have been you," it seemed to say. "If only it was you lying here and not my precious boy..."

The precious boy was shaking her by the shoulder. "Now stop that!"

Mardy stared back at him, ready to snarl out an answer. But her eye strayed beyond him, to the patch of transparent wall where the Mayor's creatures were clambering. In among the scales and feathers and claws, she saw that she was being observed. She saw eyes, round and human, calmly willing her to hate Alan, to hate herself, to give in. And she saw that she had been tricked.

She reached down inside herself, to find the place she had shrunk to. Past the resentful Mardy of this present moment. Past several other Mardys too, some of whom she now recognised for the first time. There was Mardy who'd worked so hard to make herself Queen of Fairlawn Primary School. And beyond her was the secret scoffer of Nut Krunch Bars, those chocolate-coated comforters of the soul. It was clear now, the whole shabby truth. She knew that the Mayor wanted her to see it, too, and turn in self-hatred and despair to him.

But she would not. For underneath all that self-pity and unhappiness was another Mardy the Mayor had not seen.

"You're right," she said to Alan. She got to her feet and stared boldly into the eyes of the Mayor's slave, daring them to acknowledge her. "These creatures don't look too bright, do they? We'll wait it out."

"That's the spirit, Mardy!"

She turned her hatred on the creature and concentrated it as narrowly as a laser beam. It was the slave's eyes that blinked first.

* * *

Time in Uraniborg was hard to mark, but Mardy knew they had spent a lot of it in that temple. Her own appearance had long since lost all traces of Victorian waifdom and she was now adorned, simply but nobly, in the flowing lines and draperies of imperial Rome. Unlike Alan she was not yet used to her apparel, however, and tended to lurch about the temple as if dressed in a bed sheet. Alan, meanwhile, was concentrating on a solitary game involving counters and squares, which he had discovered behind some busts in a corner of the room. Even though he was playing against himself Mardy occasionally heard him chuckle cleverly, or hiss with disgust when fooled by a move of unusual cunning. True to her resolution, she beat back her instinct to be irritated by this. Alan, she remembered, had endured Uraniborg alone far longer than she had. That couldn't have been easy, even if Dad had taught him the basics. His talent for living in a world of his own might be infuriating in ordinary life, but without it he probably wouldn't have survived.

Even now she was not finding it easy. The temple was a prison, after all. There was little to do but think, and thinking led inexorably to the past, to her own mistakes and pig-headed stupidities. Her thoughts were being continually herded in that direction, she knew, as surely as the Mayor's slaves had tried to herd her towards Uraniborg Castle. So she occupied herself in other ways – in making up rude limericks about the Mayor. She began to wonder, too, what it meant to be an Artemisian. If Alan and Rachel could do magic, did that mean she could too? She stared into her cupped hands, speculating on a form of words that would bring her weight down by fifteen pounds overnight. There didn't seem to be anything very magical in those podgy fingers, but how could she be sure? Perhaps she wouldn't have lasted this long herself but for her share of Artemisian blood.

Then there was that owl-faced, bookish man, her father. Alan had told her so much about him in the last few hours that she felt she had never known him at all. His nervous caution, his weird superstitions – how she had laughed at them once! Now they made all too much sense, as the actions of a lone Artemisian trying desperately to draw a veil over the fact of his own existence. It must have taken courage, Mardy thought, to leave the safety of Artemisia and live among ordinary people. Yet the danger she and Alan faced now was a direct result of that choice – so had he been wrong after all? She couldn't decide.

"They're gone!" Alan was suddenly hissing in her ear. "The Mayor's creatures!"

Mardy looked at the patch of transparent wall. Alan was right. She could clearly see a row of dark Victorian shop fronts, and beyond that the smoky yellow sky of Uraniborg. She got to her feet and pressed her nose to the stone. Everything outside was still. Part of an old play bill lay, as it had lain for years, undisturbed in the windless street. The very dust seemed to be sleeping.

"A bit *too* quiet?" she said uncertainly.

"Perhaps," said Alan. "Don't think it hasn't occurred to me. They may be waiting just out of sight, ready to grab us as soon as we set foot outside this temple. That's quite likely, I suppose."

"Or else they've gone back to the castle?"

"That's the other possibility."

"So which is it, Alan? No, don't answer – of course you don't know. But please guess or tell me some way we can find out, or *something*."

Alan considered. "It *feels* safe. But then it would. The Mayor's good at mood-control, you've probably noticed. If he wanted to lure us out, he'd do it just like this. An empty street, a feeling of security. The trap set and baited – what could be simpler?"

"You think we should stay put, then?" said Mardy, exasperated.

"No, I think we should go."

"But—"

"The point is, we can't know for sure. Maybe we're being led into a trap, maybe not. But we're never going to be more certain than we are right now. So we can stay in this temple for eternity – or we can take a risk." Alan smiled crookedly. "I may look good in a toga, but I know which I'd rather do."

Mardy regarded him with a kind of fearful respect. "You're positive? You know what it could mean?"

"Of course!" said Alan. He was shining with the rightness of it.

Mardy tried to protest. Suddenly it seemed desperately important that Alan should not be harmed because of her. "I'll go alone, then. If I get caught, you'll be no worse off than before."

"Mardy!" Alan laughed, but Mardy thought he looked hurt and even a little angry. "I'd never survive without you! Why do you think I hung on here so long?"

"What do you mean?"

"I hung on for you. Because I knew the Mayor would come after you, once he'd caught me. If it hadn't been for that, I'd have given in long ago."

Mardy was astonished. "You would?"

"I would, Mardy. I'm... I feel *responsible* for you."

"Oh." The word deflated Mardy at once. Responsibility was what made you do the things you didn't really want to, like washing up and homework. That must be how she made Alan feel.

Alan saw and understood. "Don't take it like that! I just mean that I love you, Spud, that's all."

"Oh... that's all right, then!" Mardy beamed. "What are we waiting for? How do we get out of this souped-up sarcophagus?"

"The same way we got in, of course. For us poor ghosts there's only one way."

He leaned against the nearest wall and Mardy was startled – although she knew she shouldn't have been – to see his shoulder and the top of his head disappear into the stonework. What was left of his face turned towards her and assumed what might in other circumstances have been a reassuring expression. He held out his hand.

"Come on, Spud, the mortar's lovely!"

Mardy got up, laughing. "You would!" She took Alan's stone-white hand in her own. The touch was neither warm nor cold, but the firm grasp was Alan's own and she suddenly felt confident that, together, they could get the better of a whole parliament of Mayors.

She pressed her fingers down into the yielding Temple marble. "Alan?"

"Yes?" Alan hesitated. "Is something wrong?"

"Nothing. Everything's perfect, or it will be soon, I hope. But all the same, Alan—"

"What?"

"Please, *please* don't call me Spud."

"WHAT WAS *THAT*?"

Hal was still staring up at the sky, which even now was in a state of convulsion. He and the Fetch were looking through the ceiling and roof of Mr Bartok's house, through plaster that had become as thin and ghostly as a reflection in a pool. Beyond, the mountainous billows of yellow cloud were a frenzy of avalanches, cascades and eruptions, but the emptiness at their centre had been more disturbing still. At times, it had swirled with images and faces that Hal recognised, in the half-blind, foolish way of dreams: faces of people whose names he had once known, each of them gazing past him with expressions of hurt betrayal. The last face had been that of Mardy herself.

Then the avalanches and eruptions had swarmed over the central void and left Hal blinking – and struck to the heart with a terrible longing for all these lost things.

So it was the Fetch who saw the pen fall.

"Hal!"

Like a slim silver bullet it lay on the floor at their feet. Or rather, it lay on Mr Bartok. It had landed on his chest, where it rose and fell with the shallow rhythm of the caretaker's breathing.

Hal looked up again. The pen had come from nowhere. A yard above his head lay a solid ceiling, textured with swirls of grimy plaster. There was no sky.

"The Mayor again?" he ventured suspiciously. Surely this was another of Mrs Mumm's tricks.

On the other hand, what need of tricks had Mrs Mumm? He and the Fetch were already her prisoners. They were stuck here with Mr Bartok, trapped by two pairs of feet convinced (whatever their brains might tell them) that they had been smuggled from other people's bodies. The pen was only a few yards away across the room, but Hal could no more have reached it than he could have touched the moon. The Fetch, however, was closer. Already she was trying to shimmy across the floor towards Mr Bartok. Her feet, still in the defiant position they had assumed when facing Mrs Mumm, stayed resolutely put – but the Fetch had somehow contrived to get to the floor and was edging her fingers closer to the caretaker. Hal heard her cry out as her ankle twisted painfully. He saw too how the discolouring of the Fetch's skin had spread all too visibly to her hands. Her nails were bruised plum-dark as she grabbed at Mr Bartok's overall and pulled it desperately towards her. There was a brief tearing and one of Mr Bartok's buttons flew to the far side of the room. Then the pen rolled lazily into the Fetch's palm.

The effect was instantaneous. At once the Fetch's feet lifted off the ground and she fell forward with her full weight on to Mr Bartok's ribs, provoking a low groan from the hapless caretaker. This the Fetch ignored, but held the pen aloft like an Olympic torch.

"Magic!" she cried. She leapt to her feet. Whatever spells Mrs Mumm had used, the touch of silver had sliced through them like butter. "Sheer magic! You realise what this means?"

"What?" asked Hal. "What does it mean?"

"It means somebody up there likes us, I hope. Someone's been sending us help."

"The Artemisians?" suggested Hal uncertainly.

"The Artemisians! You think too kindly of the Artemisians," scoffed the Fetch. "They only look out for themselves, you know."

"Perhaps – but I know they'd like us to get rid of the Mayor. Listen, I'm still stuck over here. How about letting me go now?"

"Scrapings off the same plate," muttered the Fetch as she came towards him. "Here."

Hal took the pen. As the metal touched his skin a great feeling of ease spread through him, as though he were a rusty padlock that had just been given a dose of oil. He slid one leg forward, then the other.

"You don't how wonderful that feels," he said. Then: "Ow!"

"Are you doing the hokey-cokey, Hal?"

"Pins and needles!" shouted Hal, hopping from one foot to the other.

The Fetch was still brooding on the Artemisians. "They're as bad as each other, them and the Mayor."

"Mara!"

Hal stopped in the middle of a hop and almost fell over. The voice had come from Mr Bartok. He was awake – and, though his face was putty-grey, he had propped himself up on his elbows. He stared at them with an intensity they had never thought to see on his blurry face. Whatever it was he was trying to tell them, it was desperately important that they should understand.

Which was a pity, because his words made no sense at all.

"She's a mara," he added, short of breath. "A tempter – a demon."

A gasping fit overcame him then, as if the air would not serve him to speak of the Mayor in that way. But he let his eyes become quiet and mastered it at length. "I am fighting her ban when I tell you this," he added huskily.

"Are you all right? Can you breathe?"

"Well enough," said Mr Bartok. "Must be... careful. Careless talk... costs lives."

Mr Bartok pulled himself to his feet and made it as far as a kitchen chair. All the time he had been speaking he had been eyeing Hal keenly. His eyes, which Hal had never really noticed before, did not belong to his bland, puffy, rather unhealthy face at all. They were dark and quick, and they were still trying to tell Hal something that could not be said in words. Hal believed he understood. Mrs Mumm had put Mr Bartok's tongue in detention, the same way she had fastened his own feet to the lino. Whenever Mr Bartok tried to tell Mrs Mumm's secrets, he would gag. The prohibition was strong, too – so strong that even the touch of silver was not enough to break it. Well then, if the spell could not be broken it would have to be worked round.

"Listen," he said to Mr Bartok. "Can you breathe now? So long as you don't talk too much, I mean?"

Mr Bartok gave a marginal nod.

"Good. You're saying Mrs Mumm's not human, is that it? Just nod if I'm right."

But the mention of Mrs Mumm made Mr Bartok so agitated that he could not help himself. "Pure s-spirit," he coughed, turning the word into a chaotic splutter. "Saw right away. I said, 'You're a m-m-mara'."

"How did you know?" asked the Fetch. She spoke impassively, though Mr Bartok's last effort had caused him to turn purple with the effort of breathing and Hal was afraid he would pass out again.

Despite his asphyxia, Mr Bartok somehow managed to look rather smug. He tapped his head cannily. "Psychic. Got a third eye, me. Half-Romany. See the backs of people's shadows." Now he was no longer talking about Mrs Mumm the words came easier: her ban was obviously selective.

"I saw what *you* were right away," he added to the Fetch by way of an aside.

"What do you mean by that?" demanded the Fetch belligerently.

Mr Bartok gazed at the Fetch's face, as if reassessing her. This time he did not have to fight to speak at all, though he looked deeply puzzled: "Apologies. When I first saw you I had thought you were a Fetch. Now, I'm not sure..."

"What is a mara?" interrupted Hal.

The strained look immediately came back into Mr Bartok's face and Hal at once regretted not asking a yes-no question. "Hungry spirit. Out hunting. I saw... castle – she knew..."

Hal tried to decipher these staccato revelations. "You've seen Uraniborg Castle? Where is it?"

Mr Bartok's contorted face took on an extra degree of fear. "Here... inside!" he whispered quite distinctly.

Just for a moment Hal saw it too, as if a veil had been slit. Beyond the caretaker's kitchen with its pine cupboards and cereal packets, they stood at the intersection of two vast, vaulted corridors. Such light as there was shone from the innumerable glass spy-holes posted between each pillar, but that light was dull as newsprint. Hal had never seen such a melancholy light, or watched such bales of cloth-like shadow fold themselves, ply on ply, down to desolating darkness. In that moment too he sensed the measureless weight of the halls and corridors above him and the precarious hollowed air beneath his feet. Mr Bartok's kitchen had not disappeared. It was still dimly visible through the castle walls. In a strange way, the kitchen was *part* of the castle, or of the shadow cast by its indomitable stones. And when, a moment later, the corridors faded, Hal did not feel that they had ceased to surround him. He was still walled in by their dour strength.

"You understand?" prompted Mr Bartok.

Hal nodded. Same place, different ontomorphic polarity. Hadn't Rachel said something of the kind? He hadn't understood a word of it at the time.

The Fetch, meanwhile, had been examining the silver pen rather closely – and now she unscrewed it. A scroll of paper poked out from the upper half of the casing. The Fetch removed and began to unroll it, revealing two loose sheets.

"It's a message – from Mardy," she said and handed them to Hal.

The Fetch's expression was a curious one: Hal could not tell whether she was pleased or sorry. It must be strange – very strange, he supposed – to see one's own writing and know that behind its words lay another mind and will. Perhaps the Fetch was experiencing the same kind of panic Mardy had felt when she discovered she was being stalked by her own shadow. But at least Mardy had known she was the one casting that shadow and not the other way round. Mardy had been the original, not the copy. No wonder the Fetch's smile was lopsided.

Hal read the note. It was Mardy's writing all right, down to the looped exclamation marks. She was telling Hal all about Uraniborg and the Mayor's Reverberant Chord, and begging him – if he could find a way – to play it. The chord itself was written on the other sheet. It was convoluted and cacophonous, and at first his mind reeled with the jagged complexity of it all. Mardy was asking the impossible – which was perfectly in character. All the same, as he began to examine Alan's curious notation, Hal realised that there was nothing impossible about it, really. It was fiendishly complex, that was all. With the software they had in the school music studio, for example, this chord could probably be played. Hal's mind locked on to the problem.

Both the Fetch and Mr Bartok were looking at him expectantly. But Hal was too cautious to speak his plans aloud. Mr Bartok's eyebrows seemed to be urging him to silence too. So Hal folded the paper and stuffed it casually in his pocket. He offered Mr Bartok his hand. "Are you well enough to walk?"

"I don't know where I'm going, though," said Mr Bartok, tentatively.

"And I'm not about to tell you," said Hal, beginning to pick his way back into the hall. He and Mr Bartok seemed to understand each other perfectly.

The Fetch, however, had been growing increasingly irritable.

"Tell *me*, then," she snapped.

Hal attempted to give her a meaning look. "Not *now*," he said emphatically. "It's a *secret*."

He saw that the Fetch understood quite well: he was warning her to be silent. But she chose to be obtuse. "Now!" she demanded. "I want to know what was on that piece of paper."

Hal tried to plead with her, Bartok style, using eyebrows alone. Although he could not see any cameras or microphones hidden in the caretaker's house, he guessed that whatever they said would be instantly known to the Mayor. The Fetch knew it too – but at that moment she was too angry to care. She had been getting angrier and angrier ever since she had seen Mardy's letter.

"I see what you think of me!" she blazed. "I'm just useful to you for getting your precious Mardy back. As soon as you have a sniff of her I can go hang!"

"That's not true!"

"Well, listen to this, Hal – I'm not some reversible screwdriver you can just chuck back in the toolbox when you're done with it. I'm here for keeps. And I've got more at stake here than either of you, so don't you dare think you can leave me out!"

Suddenly she had hold of Hal's collar and was twisting it into a garotte. But her face was panic-stricken. He had never seen anyone look so lonely.

"You're right," said Hal, when she relaxed her grip enough for him to speak. He knew he was taking a huge risk. But working against the Mayor ought to mean more than just outsmarting her. It ought to mean rejecting everything she stood for – like making tools of people. "We're going to the music studio," he began (though Mr Bartok's eyebrows were clamorously warning him not to). "Mardy's sent us the Mayor's Reverberant Chord and I'm going to program the computer there to play it. I think I can do it, but it will take time. And while I'm doing that," he added, looking at Mr Bartok, "I want you to rig up some heavy-duty amps. I want this chord to be heard all over Uraniborg."

"There," smiled the Fetch, dropping Hal to the floor. "That wasn't so hard to say, was it?"

Mr Bartok shook his head and moaned.

12 PARIS IN THE WINTER

THE FETCH STOOD guard just outside the new music studio, at the top of the Claines Building. Mr Bartok had let them in, then gone off looking very worried to find amplifiers and leads. He seemed convinced (though of course he was too cautious to speak of it) that the Mayor, or Mara, or whatever she was called, would appear at any moment and atomise them all.

At first Hal had expected much the same. He had been terrified crossing the playing field from Mr Dailok's house to the music studio. A dash from goalpost to goalpost, then to the shade of the industrial bins at the back of the kitchens – this had all been conspicuously furtive. But overlaying his fear, the Fetch saw, was a determination nothing would shake. His terrier face, Mardy called it, and Mardy Watt's phrases were always ready to hand. But the Fetch found now that she disagreed. There was a – a *completeness* about Hal: that was the word. He was frightened, he did not expect to succeed, yet he went on, without hesitation. He knew what was right, and he was sure of himself, as one might be sure of a rope that will take one's full weight. Hal knew who he was.

"And who am I?" the Fetch asked herself forlornly in the empty corridor.

No echo answered.

"The shadow of a ghost, that's all."

When she had first found herself in Mardy's skin the sensation had been sheer excitement, with a tang of pleasurable malice in it. The Fetch no longer remembered what her life had been before she became Mardy Watt, but she was sure she had been with a multitude of others of her kind. They had all envied human beings and despised them for the smug indifference with which they took or pushed aside life's golden opportunities. "I'll show her how living ought to be done!" That had been her first and only pure thought, before the tide of sensations and worries and desires swept in, overwhelming her with the whole messy business of being human. It all seemed very long ago.

Mr Bartok came back with an amp and sweated past her, red-faced. He and Hal were talking quietly together. "It's in two parts," Hal was saying, "activated by these two keys, see? This one, and that one after. I'm not sure I've got all the glitches out yet, so just a test run on low volume first. What? Yes, a three-minute loop should be fine."

It went on like this for some time, then they were very busy with sockets and leads and said nothing. The Fetch stopped listening.

Then came a cry from the music studio. A whoop of triumph, it seemed – but halfway through the whoop bumped up against something hard and implacable. It became more like a strangulated scream. The Fetch flew in, to find Hal with his hand still hovering over the computer keyboard. His face was white and he was straining to move his fingers stammering down towards the keys he could not quite reach. He was trying to speak to her, she thought.

At the same time, a sound swelled from the speakers: a grotesque, barbled snout of sound. It was not loud, but with it the universe seemed to reel as if from a blow. The light changed. Outside, the road from the school to the park was still visible – the Fetch could see it quite distinctly, even down to the snack wrappers drifting in the gutter. But now it was braided with another, yellower road, stretching all the way to the horizon, with a thousand lesser streets wriggling down its flanks. The sight stirred in her, not precisely a memory, but a sensation of dull, familiar horror. Her skin crawled, her guts were lead. Nameless fear – except that it had a name. *Uraniborg.*

The deserted street was no longer deserted, either. Near the castle gates was an ornate stone trough for watering horses. The two people standing beside it looked rather ghostlike, with the kerb of Bellevue Road clearly visible through their translucent bodies. They were even dressed as ghosts, in white, flowing draperies. One, a tall, slightly-built young man, was turning to his companion with a mild stoop, which made the hairs on the back of the Fetch's neck bristle with irritated recognition. His companion the Fetch could not see clearly, for she was looking away, back up the street. But the Fetch didn't need to see her face. The mere sight of Mardy Watt was enough to start the life force ebbing from her body.

Hal was still caught in suspension, his fingers quivering above the Return key, his chord only half played. That half chord swarmed about them still, tearing gaps in the light, flickering Uraniborg into existence and out again. The yellow sky darkened as a swarm of creatures lifted from the slates and turrets somewhere far above their heads. The couple by the trough looked up in astonishment and raised a deflecting cloud of yellow fog...

Hal's face was expressionless, but his eyes implored her. They might not be as eloquent as Mr Bartok's, but the Fetch knew what he meant. If she hit that Return key, the rest of the chord would play. The Mayor's power would shatter, and the Mayor's defeat would be complete.

Suddenly the Mayor was outside too. Mrs Mumm was sliding demurely through the gaps in the light. The Mara bared its tusks and roared. The two were one – the worlds cracked and shivered, but did not quite fall apart. Mardy and Alan reappeared momentarily. With one part of her mind the Fetch seemed to see Mrs Mumm upbraiding them as if she had just caught Mardy dropping litter. But her hand was raised high and the spear it held was quivering with blue ice.

And there was a jolt. Suddenly Mrs Mumm and the swarm of creatures were gone, and the Fetch could see only Mardy and Alan Watt standing uncertainly at the water trough, just as they had been when she first looked out of the window.

Hal's music seemed to be starting again, too: it must be the three-minute loop he had programmed. By now the Fetch was thoroughly confused, but she knew she must not put off pressing that key any longer. The sound of the chord was pulling at her mind like ivy at a brick wall. She put her hand to the keyboard, meaning to press it at once. But all this time a nasty thought had been pestering her for attention and now she could ignore it no longer.

Was *she* part of the world the chord was designed to obliterate?

"Why do you hesitate?" asked a voice behind her. The Fetch turned and found Rachel Fludd. Rachel was looking thinner and more sallow than ever. When she moved, the Fetch could see the potted cyclamen behind her ripple through her midriff. Rachel was carrying a hazel wand and this was the only part of her that remained steady. The rest of her body seemed solid enough in a rubbery way whenever the Fetch looked directly at it, but the solidity was tracked by a creeping disintegration and it came into her mind that Rachel Fludd was not in the room with her at all.

"You're right," said Rachel. "Most of me is still in Artemisia, trying to strengthen what's left of our borders. You and Hal have already done quite enough damage." She frowned at Hal severely, then seemed to relent, adding: "Still, as long as he is held in this suspension we may still be able to save the Mayor."

"*Save* the Mayor?" repeated the Fetch. "I thought you wanted to destroy the Mayor!"

"That was before we understood that the Mayor's Reverberant Chord was woven into Uraniborg itself," said Rachel impatiently. "That changes everything. Destroy the Mayor and you destroy the city too. We can't risk that."

The Fetch stared back in angry confusion. "Why ever not?"

"Because it borders Artemisia!" said Rachel. Even in this semi-physical form a sneer was evident in her face and voice. "All the Spells of Integrity, the Spells of Defence, they're designed to push back Uraniborg from Artemisia's borders. Without Uraniborg Artemisia itself might begin to unravel. Then there'd be nothing to separate us from the common world." On the word "common" the image of Rachel flickered with visceral disgust.

The light jolted again. Again the snout of sound poked through the threads of world and furrocked.

"Would that be such a bad thing?"

"A Fetch wouldn't understand," said Rachel rudely. Except that it was no longer Rachel. She had emerged from her disgusted flicker transformed. The Reverend Fludd now held the wand. "You are a creature of a day, Fetch," she said. "You do not know the burden of a noble and ancient lineage. Better even that Uraniborg should survive than that Artemisia should perish," she added in a Biblical voice.

"But what are you going to do with *them*?" cried the Fetch, looking at Hal's transfixed face, and at Mr Bartok, still carrying a heavy amplifier (how his muscles must ache! she thought). Though they could not move, she had no doubt that they had heard and understood all that had been said.

The Reverend Fludd considered the matter. "We can't let Hal destroy Uraniborg," she reiterated. "And he would — to save his friend he would resort to any kind of barbarism. So we shall leave him as he is. We shall leave *everything* as it is. Hal has done us all a favour, in fact. Even the Mayor is caught in this loop of time he has created. Uraniborg will never be a threat to us in this condition. You should be grateful too."

"Me? Why should I be grateful?"

"Because this way you have a chance of survival. Your only chance."

The Reverend Fludd smiled at the Fetch's miserable incomprehension.

"You are a hybrid," she explained. "You are neither of this world nor of Uraniborg. Your fate was sealed the moment the Mayor created you. If Mardy dies, you will cease to exist. If she lives to reclaim her body it will be the same."

"Stop it! I know all this!"

"But if Mardy neither lives *nor* dies – if she stays like this, repeating the same few minutes of her life for ever, then you might live too. Eternal life," repeated the Reverend Fludd piously. "Is it not what you have dreamed of?"

"Not like this!"

"Then how did you imagine it?"

"I don't know! I never thought—"

The Fetch stopped. She realised that the Reverend Fludd was not describing her – not the way she was now. She was describing the way she had been two days ago, a new-hatched cuckoo waking in Mardy Watt's nest, blindly ravenous for life. Resentful, gluttonous: a creature without a soul? Was that true? Yes, just an appetite she had been – she saw now. A bundle of appetites bound in skin.

"So leave it alone," soothed the Reverend Fludd.

"Things are best as they are. You feel sorry for Hal, don't you? I understand that. I feel sorry for him too! But I've lived so long..." and on that word it was no longer the Reverend Fludd but the Olden who spoke "...and you have lived so short a time, that neither of us can feel real kinship with him."

It was a temptation. The Felch had been born in envy, raised in skulking pretence. How she had longed to throw Mardy and Hal's humanity back in their complacent faces! And now it seemed that she alone was exempt from the loop of time that had trapped them and Uraniborg, even the Mayor, in its coils. Exempt because she was nothing, a phantom. The humans were made in *her* image now. She was alive and it was they who were reduced to stuttering reflections. And should she restore them by pressing that computer key? By extinguishing herself?

There was only one choice, really.

* * *

Alan said: "Here she comes!".

He raised his hand and yellow fog streamed from every finger. The castle began to fade, but not quickly enough to hide the figure stalking them. It was the Mayor. Mardy knew it was the Mayor, but for some reason the Mayor looked exactly like Mrs Mumm, her French teacher. Indeed, it was Mrs Mumm too. But

Mardy barely noticed: in Uraniborg appearances meant nothing. The Mayor was neither male nor female. The Mayor was It. And It was coming now, to claim her soul as its own. She looked down, half-expecting to find her body already a glistening, winged shell.

Then the music sounded – the jangling music of the Reverberant Chord. Good old Hal! she thought. I knew he could do it! The Mayor faltered. From far away came the crunch of collapsing buildings, the overthrow of whole streets. Uraniborg was falling!

But something was wrong. Several things were wrong at once. The air had blistered, and through the blisters the shape of Mardy's school was visible, but Uraniborg Castle had not disappeared. The Mayor had been hurt, but the Mayor had not disappeared either. Mrs Mumm was still advancing on them, spear in hand. And in Mardy's head there was a small, insistent voice saying: "This has happened before. This has happened before. Alan will speak now."

"I can only hear half the chord," said Alan nervously. "Your friend's botched the job."

And time juddered to a halt, horribly. Mardy could feel her blood and even her thoughts turning to treacle.

"Artemisian magic!" she heard Alan saying through blubbery lips. And he said no more. Time came to a standstill, it hovered at the brink of a slope ready to run back again, and in that awful instant of no-time Mardy saw with absolute clarity everything that had happened. The Artemisians – those ancient, bitter dregs of magic – had caught them all. The Mayor was trapped like Alan and herself in a circle of time, as monotonous as a fish bowl. They would replay the last few minutes endlessly, and each time she would understand only at the very end, and each time she would relapse into the past and forget. She would forget even what she was thinking now – *had* forgotten it probably, many times already. Unbearable!

In all this there was a small, desolate satisfaction that her dislike of Rachel Fludd had, after all, been justified.

Time teetered. Alan, as still as the Roman statue he resembled, stood with his hand in hers. The sky was drawn steely-taut overhead. The jangling half-chord played throughout, an endless backdrop to their endlessly repeated play. Mardy could feel her mind beginning to slip from her...

CRACK!

The stone trough beside her split like gunfire and a gravel of stone fragments littered her feet. That sound was the harmony to another – a bolt of noise shooting from the castle. The castle was now hardly more than a smear of grey sunlight. As Mardy blinked her eyes it was Bellevue School she saw there. It was a moment before her brain connected with her mind sufficiently to let her realise where she was.

Then she knew. That first bolt of noise was followed by others and together they were shaking the city's stones from their foundations. The missing part of the Mayor's Reverberant Chord was playing at last! And it was carrying all before it: the castle, Uraniborg, the loop of time that had lassoed them. Mrs Mumm was still on her feet, but she was staggering as she retreated to the school. All around, her world was falling.

Mardy found herself being pulled after Mrs Mumm by Alan.

"Alan!" she cried. "You don't want to catch her, do you?" Mrs Mumm might be beaten, but that meant she had nothing to lose. Weren't wounded animals the most dangerous?

"We're not after her, Mardy. We've got to find your Fetch. Don't you understand what's happening?"

"No! But whatever it is, it's bad news for the Mayor – isn't it?" panted Mardy.

"Yes, yes," said Alan impatiently. They were in the school grounds by now, running under the larch tree. A drop of misty water fell from its branches as he spoke, and hit Mardy's hand.

"Ow!" she yelped. Not quite in pain, but in shocked surprise, for the touch of that one real drop of water was heavier than anything her ghostly hand had felt since she had been in Uraniborg. She looked at her palm: it was wafering and pale, and where the water had hit it there was a ragged blurring through which the white lines of the netball court were clearly visible. "What's happening? Alan, tell me!"

"You see? We're still part of Uraniborg. If Uraniborg is destroyed, it won't just take the Mayor with it, it'll take us too. That's why we've got to find you a physical body, and fast. You're going to have to take it back from that Fetch."

Without waiting for a reply he grabbed her spectral hand and dragged her into the Claines Building. "Your Fetch is in here somewhere, I can sense it," he gasped as they reached the door, which was still ajar from Mrs Mumm's hurried entrance a moment before.

Mardy was still trying to take all this in. She had swung so often between despair and hope that she was weary of both. "But what about *your* Fetch, Alan? It's miles away, in a bed in the General Hospital. You'll never get there in time."

"Don't worry about me," said Alan. "I'll make it somehow."

With this he sped up the stairs ahead of her in a fluster of white drapery. Mardy had no choice but to follow. She could feel herself fading, the ghostliness of her legs all too obvious as they laboured up the harsh metal steps of the Claines Building. She had little idea what she would find, but she knew that this was not what she had planned for herself. Her ambitions had never been grandiose, but she had not thought she would end her days an out-of-breath, dishevelled, temporary ghost.

Finally she made the studio corridor. It was worth the effort, if only to see Hal and Mr Bartok grappling Mrs Mumm – or what was left of her – to the ground, just outside the studio door. Mrs Mumm was squawking like a parrot, and screaming unspeakable things in French. Mardy found an even more startling scene in the studio itself. There was Mardy Watt – no! the Fetch, she corrected herself – giving Rachel Fludd a series of expert right hooks, while Alan looked on in obvious astonishment. Considering that Rachel was only half there the Fetch's punches were remarkably effective. Rachel crumpled backwards into a filing cabinet, helpless with fury.

Then she saw Mardy. "You've done it now," Rachel cried hoarsely to the Fetch. Her battered face assumed a smirk of triumph. "See, Mardy Watt has come to take her property back!"

She raised her arm and made a circular motion with the hand that held the wand. The wand flickered and in its wake a luminous blackness began to manifest itself above her head. Finally, Rachel's body seemed to dissolve and swirl into the blackness, like dirty water going down a plughole. And she was not there any more.

"Where did *she* disappear to?" asked Mardy.

"Back to Artemisia, I'd guess," said Alan. "What's

left of it. She opened an ontomorphic portal – look. An Artemisian can get anywhere through one of those."

"An ontomorphic portal? Is that one of the basics Dad taught you?"

Alan did not wait to reply. "I'd better hitch a ride before it fades out. I've got an appointment at the hospital. Good luck, Mardy! Hug a Fetch today!"

With that, he made a kind of twisting leap up towards the disc of blackness, which was still hovering faintly where Rachel Fludd had been standing. As he left the ground his body thinned and streamed out in black and purple lines, until a moment later all that was visible of him was a helix of quivering energy. It pushed through the fading portal just before it disappeared entirely, with a faint pop and a spatter of sulphur.

But Mardy did not have time to stand watching. Hal and Mr Bartok had succeeded in restraining Mrs Mumm. Mr Bartok was sitting on her stomach, while Mrs Mumm, in a final spurt of desperate magic, transformed herself into terrifying and repellent forms. She became, in quick succession, a grizzly bear, a giant scorpion, a leech and a red-hot poker. But nothing would move Mr Bartok. He just sat on her with all his fifteen-stone weight and shouted: "Mara, mara! We got you now, eh?" – just like a playground bully. At last, she seemed to give up the fight. Her body went limp. Hal, hovering beside Mr Bartok, was asking uncertainly: "Is she dead?" He did not seem to have noticed Mardy at all.

And that, Mardy realised, was natural, because she was still a ghost. Whatever Rachel Fludd might see, to Hal and other humans she was still invisible. Just then she glimpsed her reflection in one of the computer screens. It was hardly there. The dreadful translucence she had begun to acquire with the fall of Uraniborg had advanced until now she was hardly more than a blotch of walking colour. Soon she would be nothing but a mind, a mood blown about with every breeze. The blotch of colour in the mirror slackened into horror and the remains of a face she dimly knew to be her own reflected back her blurry misery.

Claim your body from the Fetch, Alan had said. But he had not stayed long enough to tell her how. She could see the Fetch now, crouching in the corner after its battle with Rachel. It looked to her like more like a wild animal than a human being. Its eyes were red, its skin discoloured with what might have been either dirt or bruising, its hair – despite Mardy's dutiful brushing, morning and night – was matted and stiff. Worst of all, the Fetch was now coming across the carpet to where she stood. A Fetch's eyes, it seemed, were sharp enough to spot a dissolving ghost. Its arms were outstretched and the expression on its face was that of a cadaver, half grin, half snarl – insatiable. Mardy wanted to run, to scream – but could move neither hand nor foot. The Fetch was right before her now, its face almost touching her own. What did it want, Mardy asked herself? What last insult did it mean to fling at her?

"Don't be afraid," breathed the Fetch.

Mardy was too surprised to react. Perhaps it was the effect of hearing her own voice speaking with such tenderness – but as the Fetch's arms closed about her she felt no fear, only a trembling intimacy with the other mind that had shared her body. A mind so different from her imagination of it that she felt for a moment as if *she* was the Fetch, and this strange-familiar other the true Mardy. Then came a dreary, insensible time of waiting and finally the claggy weight of her own limbs as she fell, and rapped her head on the edge of a table in doing so.

She must have been out cold for a minute because when she woke – and it was an effort to do so – she found Mr Bartok and Hal crouched beside her. Someone (no doubt Hal, who knew about such things) had put her in the recovery position, on her side with one leg bent. Her head hurt where she had cracked it.

"I'm OK," she muttered. "Don't crowd me." Even the use of her tongue was strange: it flopped about inside her mouth like a landed trout. Hal put his hand on the back of her own. The touch of Hal's warm, soft hand, the sound of Mr Bartok's voice asking what had happened, even the smell of the new studio carpet on which she was lying, overwhelmed her senses, grown feeble by the weightless, joyless, quarter-life of Uraniborg. The last few minutes seemed a bit muddled. If only her head did not hurt so much...

"I'm all right," she said, answering what she thought Mr Bartok had just asked her. "I just fell. Oh, Hal, I'm so glad to see you!"

"I haven't gone anywhere," Hal replied, a little puzzled. "You're the one who was in danger, not us. Mr Bartok was great – he knew exactly how to handle Mrs Mumm."

"Once you have hold of her you must never let go," explained Mr Bartok. "And don't let her use the mind magic on you, that's the trick. Think of sauerkraut and old socks, anything – don't let the fear inside your brain!"

"But you," said Hal to Mardy, "you had Rachel to deal with! And you did it the last way she was expecting."

"But that wasn't... I didn't," began Mardy.

"She was expecting a wizard's duel, not a thump on the nose. I wish I could have watched it!"

"*I* didn't hit anyone," said Mardy. The truth was beginning to dawn on her and it was not pleasant. "That wasn't me. That was the Fetch."

"What did you say?" Hal looked confused.

"Don't you see, Hal? I'm back. I'm Mardy. The Fetch isn't here any more. We've beaten the Mayor. We've won!"

Mardy stopped. "Hal? What's the matter with you?"

"Nothing," he mumbled. "You sure you're OK?" He peered into her eyes, as if looking for something.

"After what's happened to me, I don't think I'll ever be sure of anything again. What's wrong, Hal? Tell me!"

"I'm glad, very glad," said Hal. "I thought you were lost for good."

"You could look a bit more pleased about it."

"I am, Mardy! You have to believe me – I've thought about nothing else but getting you back ever since you spoke to me in the playground. It's just, if you're *here* – what's happened to the Fetch?"

"Hal, I don't know! Why would anything have happened to it? It was only ever built to last a few days, you know that. Do you care?"

"Well..."

"You do! You do care!" cried Mardy in outrage. "You like that monster better than me!"

"It changed, Mardy! When it began, it was like an animal – a machine. All it wanted was to take over your life. It didn't feel for anyone."

"And now? It's giving up its evenings to do charity work, is it?" said Mardy.

"Not exactly. It just wants to be human, I think."

"Well, it isn't!" said Mardy ferociously. Then she remembered the voice that had embraced her, telling her not to be afraid, and the brief tenderness of her contact with the mind behind that voice. She added quietly: "It wasn't. I'm sorry, Hal."

"She wasn't just a candle to be snuffed out. She deserved more than that."

"A very touching scene!" said a clear voice from the far side of the room. Hal and Mardy knew it at once. They had heard it twice a week since the previous September, teaching them the days of the week and correcting their irregular French verbs.

Mrs Mumm was on her feet again. There was a cry of astonishment from Mr Bartok, but she poked him back with a stab of her elegant finger. "You look like you've seen a ghost," she laughed sarcastically.

"What do you want?" stammered Hal. A few moments before he had seen Mrs Mumm's body lifeless on the carpet. Yet she had never looked so alive, so animated as she did now. He had never seen that expression on her face, either. It reminded him of something. Of someone...

"Is that *you*?" he said, squinting at her face as if he could see through it to the soul within. "Are you Mardy's Fetch?"

"I *was* a Fetch," came the reply. "I don't think I'm one now."

"You mean – you've become real?"

"I was always real," corrected the Fetch. "As real as you, Hal Young. Only now I have a body of my own to prove it."

Mr Bartok was suddenly bursting to speak. "I saw it! I saw your spirit flit – a streak in the air, just before you collapsed!"

"You do have sharp eyes after all," said the Fetch. "Yes, I left Mardy's body just in time, I think." She gave Mardy a gracious smile. "It's not such a bad body, Mardy, and thank you for the loan of it."

"Don't mention it," muttered Mardy, looking at the blotches on her hands with resignation.

"Then I was outside again. No skin to hide behind, just raw consciousness. And I remembered how I had been that way before, in Uraniborg – when the Mayor kept us flocking in the caves of his castle and there was no hiding place, just the bell, the rough stone, the Mayor's scorching eye..." The Fetch's voice filled and choked a little. Then she looked down briskly at herself and smiled. "So I knew what to do. I had to find a new home, one nobody could take from me. And I knew where I could find it."

"From the Mayor, you mean? And is the Mayor quite dead?" Mr Bartok seemed very anxious on this point.

"There *was* something here. A shrivelled, worn-out heart and a soul to match. But when you played the Reverberant Chord, Hal, you broke that heart. It had no power to resist me. It fled."

A strange sensation now came over Mardy. It was as if someone, somewhere, were trying very feebly to tell her what to think. "Feel sorry for me!" it commanded pleadingly. "Feel pity for the Mayor!" Only there was no force behind it – Mardy shook it off as easily as a fallen leaf. She felt no pity at all.

"I don't know what to call you," Hal was saying to the Fetch. His face was shining with a kind of wary, amazed joy. "Are we going to call you Mrs Mumm or what?"

"You certainly will not! I'll choose my own name, thank you. I've earned that privilege. From now on," announced the Fetch grandly, "my name is Florimell Anastasia Crawford Garbo."

The way she said it, no one could doubt that Florimell Anastasia Crawford Garbo was indeed her name – and no one else's.

"But you can call me Flossie," she added kindly.

* * *

Mr Bartok did not accompany them as they left the school. The state of the music studio had begun to grieve his caretaker's heart. One of the pot plants had got knocked over in the fight with Rachel Fludd, and before Mardy, Hal and Flossie left he was already plugging in the vacuum cleaner.

"Good luck to you," he said, shaking Flossie vigorously by the hand and arm. "I am glad Mrs Mumm is no longer lying dead here on my new carpet."

"Glad to be of service," said Flossie Garbo.

"But be careful," he added darkly. "She still may be capable of something."

"We will," said Hal.

For all that, Mardy did not think Hal believed Mrs Mumm to be capable of anything now. And that worried her a little, because the feeble voice was still there, somewhere nearby, cajoling her with its demands for pity.

All this time the Reverberant Chord had been playing on. Even when Hal turned off the computer its echo rumbled like thunder across the farther districts of Uraniborg. As they stepped out of the Claines Building, the sound was blended into the engines and birdsong of Bellevue Road, and the urgent siren of an ambulance heading down Mersea Hill towards The Butts. Before many seconds had passed none of them could distinguish it from any other sound, but underneath the Reverberant Chord did not stop playing.

"What will you do, Flossie?" Hal asked. "Mrs Mumm must have a house somewhere, a family. A Mr Mumm, come to that. Are you just going to slot into her life like you did with Mardy's? How's your French?"

"I didn't have a choice about Mardy. I didn't know any better, either. But you're wrong about Mrs Mumm. The French teacher act was just a loophole to give her a place in this world. Her real life was in Uraniborg."

"But I used to see her drive off in that red hatchback every day after school," protested Mardy. "We all did."

"And what happened when she turned the corner? She wasn't going home to put her feet up and watch the soaps, I bet – and I don't believe in Mr Mumm, either."

"How can you be so sure?" asked Hal.

"If you'd ever been a Fetch yourself, you'd understand," said Flossie condescendingly. "When I first entered Mardy's life there was hardly room to breathe for all the memories and appetites and prejudices. It was all 'How can I lose four pounds this month?' and 'Where did I put my library books?' and 'Why does Mum go on at me to clean under my nails?'"

"We get the point," said Mardy stiffly.

"What I mean is, Mardy was a real person," smiled Flossie. "But now it's like I've moved into one of those show homes. It's empty and squeaky clean and no one's ever sat on the toilet, but it's got no *soul*. Until I came along, that is. Take it from me, there is no Mrs Mumm."

"So what are you going to do – with no identity, no house, no money?"

"Who says I have no identity? I'm Florimell Anastasia Crawford Garbo and the world will have to take me as it can. After everything that's happened, do you really think I'm worried because I haven't got a low-cost mortgage? I'm going to see some life and live it too."

Thunder was gnawing at the horizon. Occasionally Mardy could hear a stray echo of the Reverberant Chord as it patrolled and repatrolled the town's borders. There were more sirens, too – police and fire as well as several ambulances, heading down towards The Butts, where they were laying down a thick sediment of stress and sound. The spells that had fixed the Artemisian boundary with Uraniborg were whipping back like cut hawsers, creating who-knew-what destruction in the process. Mardy hoped it would not be trivial.

Flossie said, as if reading her mind. "I don't think you'll be seeing Rachel Fludd at school next week. She'll be needed at home."

"That's fine by me."

"How many of these Artemisians are there, anyway?" puzzled Hal. "I only saw three close up and even they seemed to be the same person half the time."

"I don't think the Artemisians have much use for the idea of people," said Flossie. "Not the way you mean, all separate like grains of sand. They only see the beach. You might as well ask how many clouds there are in the sky."

Mardy wondered if that was why her father had left Artemisia. All this gliding and sliding of one person into another struck her as rather undignified. "No one's splitting me up into little bits again, *ever*," she said vehemently.

"I don't think anyone would dare try," said Hal.

Pity the Mayor, pity poor Mrs Mumm! Let her out, unshackle her poor limbs!

Even Hal felt it this time.

"Did somebody say something?" he asked. "I could have sworn I heard Mrs Mumm's voice."

"You did," said Mardy. "It was coming from your pocket."

She reached into Hal's coat. Her hand closed upon a round object, about the size and shape of a tennis ball. As she drew it out, she was aware of a faint liquid motion.

"So that's where she got to!"

It was the snowstorm souvenir Hal had picked up in Mr Bartok's house. There was the Eiffel Tower, caught in a blizzard — and beside it a plastic Parisienne enjoying the snow. But the Parisienne's face was no formless blob of moulded plastic. It was Mrs Mumm's and she was chattering with cold.

"I suppose she had nowhere else to go after I evicted her," commented Flossie. "Any port in a snowstorm."

"Poor thing!" said Hal, staring at Mrs Mumm compassionately.

"Don't you believe it," said Mardy. "She's making you feel that. You should know the way she operates by now."

"Even so..."

"Enough!" cried Mardy. "I'd better take this off your hands or she'll be out again and setting up Uraniborg the Second by Monday morning."

She took the snow storm and shook it, hard. Was it her imagination, or were the plastic Mrs Mumm's hands and nose tinged blue with cold as the flakes of liquid snow drifted about her legs? That yellow dress was quite inadequate for the weather, of course. Mardy examined herself for signs of pity, as she might check a collar for stray hairs. She found none and was satisfied.

"What are you going to do with it?" asked Hal anxiously.

"Keep it. On my desk, probably. It'll make a good paperweight."

"Aren't you afraid she'll – you know – find a way of escaping?"

"I'll keep my eye on her. She's had her eye on me long enough. Oh, don't look so worried, Hal! I'm not totally helpless. I'm half-Artemisian myself, you know," she added rather haughtily.

"It shows," said Hal.

"Besides, I can always ask— Oh my goodness!"

"What is it?"

"I must get home at once!" cried Mardy. "I've got to know what happened to Alan!"

They hurried up Bellevue Road and through the park, skirting the War Memorial and a number of drunks on the way. When they reached Mardy's house, Mrs Watt was already outside and just about to climb into the car. If she was surprised to see Mardy and Hal with one of their teachers, she did not show it. In fact, she was too excited to notice anything.

"Thank goodness you're here, Mardy! We've got to get to the hospital."

"Why?" cried Mardy. "What's wrong?"

"Nothing! Quite the opposite. They just rang to say there's been a – a change, in Alan's condition."

"He's woken up? He's going to be all right?"

"Don't get carried away, Mardy! Let's just say they want us there. Now, Mardy!"

Mrs Watt ran round to the driver's door. She was more than a little carried away herself. She looked back, taking in Flossie properly for the first time. "You're one of Mardy's teachers, aren't you? Mrs Mumm?"

"Actually," began Flossie, "my name is Florimell Anastasia—"

"Yes! She met us in town and gave us a lift back. Thanks, Miss."

"Yes, thank you!" enthused Mardy's mother. "You couldn't have come along at a better time."

Mardy noticed Hal hovering. "Can Hal come too, Mum?"

"Of course – but do get in!"

As Mrs Watt strapped herself in, Mardy and Flossie stood on the pavement, facing each other shyly.

"Your brother will be fine, I'm sure of it," said Flossie.

"Will I ever see you again?" asked Mardy.

"Not in the mirror, I promise you!" Flossie replied. "I want to get some memories of my own, first. But watch the skies, Mardy, and who knows?" She smiled a self-mocking smile that was all her own. "After all, I've grown accustomed to your face."

"Mardy!" called her mother.

"Coming!"

"Oh, and Hal?" added Flossie.

"What? Aagh!"

Hal had never thought to find himself being given a bear-hug by his French teacher, still less by a Fetch. But then, he thought as she let him drop and the breath returned to his body, it isn't really either of them. It's Flossie. Not knowing her own strength is just part of what she's like.

"Good luck," he gasped hoarsely.

The car door slammed, Mrs Watt revved the engine and was gone. Flossie watched them turn the corner, then doubled back and followed the road Hal had taken the day before, from Mardy's house to Mersea Hill. There she stopped and checked her pockets. She found a gold bracelet, a few coins and four twenty-pound notes. Mrs Mumm was obviously the kind of sensible demon who liked to keep some ready cash about her. Flossie scrutinised the world from the top of the slope. Beyond the inky line of the river the fields had been quilted and laid flat, down to a range of tranquil and inviting hills. Surely there was room in all that vastness for one resourceful ex-Fetch to find a place called home?

"*Bien sûr,*" she said out loud. "*N'aies pas peur.*" Whatever her other misdeeds, Mrs Mumm seemed to have bequeathed her a good working knowledge of French. That would be useful, too. London first, she decided, to make some money – then the Channel. What about a passport? Clothes? Time enough, she thought, for all these things. As she descended the hill, questions and worries floated round her head like cherubim and were luxurious. Flossie was quite content.

By now she had reached The Butts. The entrance to the street smelt of sulphur and the pavement was black with charred spells, but the fire engines and ambulances had gone. It occurred to her that there was a duty to be performed here and that no one but she would do it. Flossie licked her finger and poked it over the border into Artemisia. There was resistance, but no more than if she were pushing through a cobweb. The Artemisians, bunkered behind glass, watched resentfully as she strode up the street. The spire at its far end did not stray. A small boy was playing in the front garden of one of the houses. He had a toy gun.

"*Thwat, thwat, thwat!*"

Flossie gave him a smooth, invulnerable smile as she passed. At her back, she heard the boy's mother rush out of the house, scolding. A door slammed.

Flossie Anastasia Crawford Garbo continued down the long, straight street to the Church of St Thomas the Doubter. There she stepped into the stone-cool darkness, and breathed the lily-scented air. She lit a candle and thought of all those souls enslaved by the Mayor of Uraniborg, and extinguished with the fall of that city. She thought of what her own fate had once been and wept.

Then she put her handkerchief back in her pocket and dropped a coin into the box. And she asked whatever gods were there to grant her a fair journey.

Calypso, Dreaming

CHARLES BUTLER

Calypso tucked her knees together and hooked her hands round her shins. Other people, she had begun to learn, had dreams that stayed dreams. They were lucky, those people. Her dreams always came true.

The isle of Sweetholm seems like the perfect retreat. A haven for wildlife, its near-isolation means it is just too far away from the mainland to attract the hordes of daytrippers that swarm to the beach at the first sign of summer. Tansy, in particular, is looking forward to spending the holidays there. It's a chance to escape the mess back home, where her experiments in magic went so horribly wrong.

But troubles cannot be so easily outrun, for beneath Sweetholm's idyllic exterior seethes a darker heart...